I0615789

Reprint Publishing

FOR PEOPLE WHO GO FOR ORIGINALS.

www.reprintpublishing.com

" ' WELCOME TO BANGLETOP ' "

The Water Ghost
and Others

BY

JOHN KENDRICK BANGS
AUTHOR OF "COFFEE AND REPARTEE"

ILLUSTRATED

NEW YORK
HARPER & BROTHERS PUBLISHERS
1894

By JOHN KENDRICK BANGS.

COFFEE AND REPARTEE.
THREE WEEKS IN POLITICS.

Illustrated. 32mo, Cloth, Ornamental, 50 cents each.

PUBLISHED BY HARPER & BROTHERS, NEW YORK.

☞ *For sale by all booksellers, or will be sent by the publishers, postage prepaid, to any part of the United States, Canada, or Mexico, on receipt of price.*

Copyright, 1894, by HARPER & BROTHERS.

All rights reserved.

TO

FRANCIS SEDGWICK BANGS

CONTENTS

ILLUSTRATIONS

THE WATER GHOST OF HAR-
ROWBY HALL

THE trouble with Harrowby Hall was
that it was haunted, and, what was worse,
the ghost did not content itself with merely
appearing at the bedside of the afflicted
person who saw it, but persisted in remaining there for one mortal hour before it
would disappear.

It never appeared except on Christmas
Eve, and then as the clock was striking
twelve, in which respect alone was it lack-
ing in that originality which in these days
is a *sine qua non* of success in spectral life.
The owners of Harrowby Hall had done
their utmost to rid themselves of the damp
and dewy lady who rose up out of the
best bedroom floor at midnight, but without avail. They had tried stopping the
clock, so that the ghost would not know

when it was midnight; but she made her appearance just the same, with that fearful miasmatic personality of hers, and there she would stand until everything about her was thoroughly saturated.

Then the owners of Harrowby Hall calked up every crack in the floor with the very best quality of hemp, and over this were placed layers of tar and canvas; the walls were made water-proof, and the doors and windows likewise, the proprietors having conceived the notion that the unexorcised lady would find it difficult to leak into the room after these precautions had been taken; but even this did not suffice. The following Christmas Eve she appeared as promptly as before, and frightened the occupant of the room quite out of his senses by sitting down alongside of him and gazing with her cavernous blue eyes into his; and he noticed, too, that in her long, aqueously bony fingers bits of dripping sea-weed were entwined, the ends hanging down, and these ends she drew across his forehead until he became like one insane. And then he swooned away, and was found unconscious in his bed the next morning by his host, simply saturated with sea-water and fright, from the combined effects of which he never recovered, dying four years later of pneumonia and nervous prostration at the age of seventy-eight.

The next year the master of Harrowby Hall decided not to have the best spare bedroom opened at all, thinking that perhaps the ghost's thirst for making herself disagreeable would be satisfied by haunting the furniture, but the plan was as unavailing as the many that had preceded it.

The ghost appeared as usual in the room — that is, it was supposed she did, for the hangings were dripping wet the next morning, and in the parlor below the haunted room a great damp spot appeared on the ceiling. Finding no one there, she immediately set out to learn the reason why, and she chose none other to haunt than the owner of the Harrowby himself. She found him in his own cosey room drinking whiskey—whiskey undiluted—and felicitating himself upon having foiled her ghostship, when all of a sudden the curl

went out of his hair, his whiskey bottle
filled and overflowed, and he was himself
in a condition similar to that of a man who
has fallen into a water-butt. When he recovered from the shock, which was a pain-
ful one, he saw before him the lady of the
cavernous eyes and sea-weed fingers. The
sight was so unexpected and so terrifying
that he fainted, but immediately came to,
because of the vast amount of water in his
hair, which, trickling down over his face,
restored his consciousness.

Now it so happened that the master of
Harrowby was a brave man, and while he
was not particularly fond of interviewing
ghosts, especially such quenching ghosts
as the one before him, he was not to be
daunted by an apparition. He had paid
the lady the compliment of fainting from
the effects of his first surprise, and now
that he had come to he intended to find
out a few things he felt he had a right to
know. He would have liked to put on a
dry suit of clothes first, but the apparition
declined to leave him for an instant until
her hour was up, and he was forced to deny

himself that pleasure. Every time he would move she would follow him, with the result that everything she came in contact with got a ducking. In an effort to warm himself up he approached the fire, an unfortunate move as it turned out, because it brought the ghost directly over the fire, which immediately was extinguished. The whiskey became utterly valueless as a comforter to his chilled system, because it was by this time diluted to a proportion of ninety per cent. of water. The only thing he could do to ward off the evil effects of his encounter he did, and that was to swallow ten two-grain quinine pills, which he managed to put into his mouth before the ghost had time to interfere. Having done this, he turned with some asperity to the ghost, and said :

"Far be it from me to be impolite to a woman, madam, but I'm hanged if it wouldn't please me better if you'd stop these infernal visits of yours to this house. Go sit out on the lake, if you like that sort of thing; soak the water-butt, if you wish; but do not, I implore you, come into a gentleman's house and saturate him and his possessions in this way. It is damned disagreeable."

"Henry Hartwick Oglethorpe," said the ghost, in a gurgling voice, "you don't know what you are talking about."

"Madam," returned the unhappy householder, "I wish that remark were strictly truthful. I was talking about you. It would be shillings and pence—nay, pounds, in my pocket, madam, if I did not know you."

"That is a bit of specious nonsense," returned the ghost, throwing a quart of indignation into the face of the master of Harrowby. "It may rank high as repartee, but as a comment upon my statement that you do not know what you are talking about, it savors of irrelevant impertinence. You do not know that I am compelled to haunt this place year after year by inexorable fate. It is no pleasure to me to enter this house, and ruin and mildew everything I touch. I never aspired to be a showerbath, but it is my doom. Do you know who I am?"

"No, I don't," returned the master of Harrowby. "I should say you were the Lady of the Lake, or Little Sallie Waters."

"You are a witty man for your years," said the ghost.

"Well, my humor is drier than yours ever will be," returned the master.

"No doubt. I'm never dry. I am the Water Ghost of Harrowby Hall, and dryness is a quality entirely beyond my wildest hope. I have been the incumbent of this highly unpleasant office for two hundred years to-night."

"How the deuce did you ever come to get elected?" asked the master.

"Through a suicide," replied the spectre. "I am the ghost of that fair maiden whose picture hangs over the mantel-piece in the drawing-room. I should have been your great-great-great-great-great-aunt if I had lived, Henry Hartwick Oglethorpe, for I was the own sister of your great-great-great-great-grandfather."

"But what induced you to get this house into such a predicament?"

"I was not to blame, sir," returned the

lady. "It was my father's fault. He it was who built Harrowby Hall, and the haunted chamber was to have been mine. My father had it furnished in pink and yellow, knowing well that blue and gray formed the only combination of color I could tolerate. He did it merely to spite me, and, with what I deem a proper spirit, I declined to live in the room; whereupon my father said I could live there or on the lawn, he didn't care which. That night I ran from the house and jumped over the cliff into the sea."

"That was rash," said the master of Harrowby.

"So I've heard," returned the ghost. "If I had known what the consequences were to be I should not have jumped; but I really never realized what I was doing until after I was drowned. I had been drowned a week when a sea-nymph came to me and informed me that I was to be one of her followers forever afterwards, adding that it should be my doom to haunt Harrowby Hall for one hour every Christmas Eve throughout the rest of eternity. I was to haunt that room on such Christmas Eves as I found it inhabited; and if it should turn out not to be inhabited, I was and am to spend the allotted hour with the head of the house."

" I'll sell the place."

" That you cannot do, for it is also required of me that I shall appear as the deeds are to be delivered to any purchaser, and divulge to him the awful secret of the house."

" Do you mean to tell me that on every Christmas Eve that I don't happen to have somebody in that guest-chamber, you are going to haunt me wherever I may be, ruining my whiskey, taking all the curl out of my hair, extinguishing my fire, and soaking me through to the skin?" demanded the master.

" You have stated the case, Oglethorpe. And what is more," said the water ghost, " it doesn't make the slightest difference where you are, if I find that room empty, wherever you may be I shall douse you with my spectral pres—"

Here the clock struck one, and immediately the apparition faded away. It was

perhaps more of a trickle than a fade, but
as a disappearance it was complete.

"By St. George and his Dragon!" ejaculated the master of Harrowby, wringing his
hands. "It is guineas to hot-cross buns
that next Christmas there's an occupant of
the spare room, or I spend the night in a
bath-tub."

But the master of Harrowby would have
lost his wager had there been any one there
to take him up, for when Christmas Eve
came again he was in his grave, never
having recovered from the cold contracted
that awful night. Harrowby Hall was closed,
and the heir to the estate was in London,
where to him in his chambers came the
same experience that his father had gone
through, saving only that, being younger
and stronger, he survived the shock. Everything in his rooms was ruined — his
clocks were rusted in the works ; a fine collection of water-color drawings was entirely obliterated by the onslaught of the water
ghost; and what was worse, the apartments
below his were drenched with the water
soaking through the floors, a damage for

which he was compelled to pay, and which resulted in his being requested by his landlady to vacate the premises immediately.

The story of the visitation inflicted upon his family had gone abroad, and no one could be got to invite him out to any function save afternoon teas and receptions. Fathers of daughters declined to permit him to remain in their houses later than eight o'clock at night, not knowing but that some emergency might arise in the supernatural world which would require the unexpected appearance of the water ghost in this on nights other than Christmas Eve, and before the mystic hour when weary churchyards, ignoring the rules which are supposed to govern polite society, begin to yawn. Nor would the maids themselves have aught to do with him, fearing the destruction by the sudden incursion of aqueous femininity of the costumes which they held most dear.

So the heir of Harrowby Hall resolved, as his ancestors for several generations before him had resolved, that something must be done. His first thought was to make

one of his servants occupy the haunted
room at the crucial moment; but in this
he failed, because the servants themselves
knew the history of that room and rebelled.
None of his friends would consent to sacri-
fice their personal comfort to his, nor was
there to be found in all England a man so
poor as to be willing to occupy the doomed
chamber on Christmas Eve for pay.

Then the thought came to the heir to
have the fireplace in the room enlarged, so
that he might evaporate the ghost at its
first appearance, and he was felicitating
himself upon the ingenuity of his plan, when
he remembered what his father had told
him—how that no fire could withstand the
lady's extremely contagious dampness. And
then he bethought him of steam - pipes.
These, he remembered, could lie hundreds
of feet deep in water, and still retain suffi-
cient heat to drive the water away in vapor;
and as a result of this thought the haunted
room was heated by steam to a withering degree, and the heir for six months at-
tended daily the Turkish baths, so that
when Christmas Eve came he could himself

withstand the awful temperature of the room.

The scheme was only partially successful. The water ghost appeared at the specified time, and found the heir of Harrowby prepared; but hot as the room was, it shortened her visit by no more than five minutes in the hour, during which time the nervous system of the young master was wellnigh shattered, and the room itself was cracked and warped to an extent which required the outlay of a large sum of money to remedy. And worse than this, as the last drop of the water ghost was slowly sizzling itself out on the floor, she whispered to her would-be conqueror that his scheme would avail him nothing, because there was still water in great plenty where she came from, and that next year would find her rehabilitated and as exasperatingly saturating as ever.

It was then that the natural action of the mind, in going from one extreme to the other, suggested to the ingenious heir of Harrowby the means by which the water ghost was ultimately conquered, and happi-

ness once more came within the grasp of
the house of Oglethorpe.

The heir provided himself with a warm
suit of fur under-clothing.   Donning this
with the furry side in, he placed over it
a rubber garment, tightfitting, which he
wore just as a woman wears a jersey.   On
top of this he placed another set of under-clothing, this suit made of wool, and
over this was a second rubber garment
like the first.   Upon his head he placed
a light and comfortable diving helmet,
and so clad, on the following Christmas
Eve he awaited the coming of his tor-
mentor.

It was a bitterly cold night that brought
to a close this twenty-fourth day of Decem-
ber.   The air outside was still, but the temperature was below zero.   Within all was
quiet, the servants of Harrowby Hall await-
ing with beating hearts the outcome of their
master's campaign against his supernatural
visitor.

The master himself was lying on the bed
in the haunted room, clad as has already
been indicated, and then—

The clock clanged out the hour of twelve.

There was a sudden banging of doors, a blast of cold air swept through the halls, the door leading into the haunted chamber flew open, a splash was heard, and the water ghost was seen standing at the side of the heir of Harrowby, from whose outer dress there streamed rivulets of water, but whose own person deep down under the various garments he wore was as dry and as warm as he could have wished.

" Ha !" said the young master of Harrowby. "I'm glad to see you."

" You are the most original man I've met, if that is true," returned the ghost. "May I ask where did you get that hat ?"

" Certainly, madam," returned the master, courteously. "It is a little portable observatory I had made for just such emergencies as this. But, tell me, is it true that you are doomed to follow me about for one mortal hour—to stand where I stand, to sit where I sit ?"

" That is my delectable fate," returned the lady.

"We'll go out on the lake," said the master, starting up.

"You can't get rid of me that way," returned the ghost. "The water won't swallow me up ; in fact, it will just add to my present bulk."

"Nevertheless," said the master, firmly, "we will go out on the lake."

"But, my dear sir," returned the ghost, with a pale reluctance, "it is fearfully cold out there. You will be frozen hard before you've been out ten minutes."

"Oh no, I'll not," replied the master. "I am very warmly dressed. Come !" This last in a tone of command that made the ghost ripple.

And they started.

They had not gone far before the water ghost showed signs of distress.

"You walk too slowly," she said. "I am nearly frozen. My knees are so stiff now I can hardly move. I beseech you to accelerate your step."

"I should like to oblige a lady," returned the master, courteously, "but my clothes are rather heavy, and a hundred yards an

hour is about my speed.   Indeed, I think
we would better sit down here on this snow-
drift, and talk matters over."

"Do not!   Do not do so, I beg!" cried
the ghost.   "Let me move on.   I feel myself growing rigid as it is.   If we stop here,
I shall be frozen stiff."

"That, madam," said the master slowly,
and seating himself on an ice-cake—"that
is why I have brought you here.   We have
been on this spot just ten minutes; we have
fifty more.   Take your time about it, madam,
but freeze, that is all I ask of you."

"I cannot move my right leg now," cried
the ghost, in despair, "and my overskirt is a
solid sheet of ice.   Oh, good, kind Mr. Oglethorpe, light a fire, and let me go free from
these icy fetters."

"Never, madam.   It cannot be.   I have
you at last."

"Alas!" cried the ghost, a tear trickling
down her frozen cheek.   "Help me, I beg.
I congeal!"

"Congeal, madam, congeal!" returned
Oglethorpe, coldly.   "You have drenched
me and mine for two hundred and three

years, madam. To-night you have had your last drench."

"Ah, but I shall thaw out again, and then you'll see. Instead of the comfortably tepid, genial ghost I have been in my past, sir, I shall be iced - water," cried the lady, threateningly.

"No, you won't, either," returned Ogle-thorpe; "for when you are frozen quite stiff, I shall send you to a cold-storage warehouse, and there shall you remain an icy work of art forever more."

"But warehouses burn."

"So they do, but this warehouse cannot burn. It is made of asbestos and surrounding it are fire-proof walls, and within those walls the temperature is now and shall forever be 416 degrees below the zero point; low enough to make an icicle of any flame in this world—or the next," the master added, with an ill-suppressed chuckle.

"For the last time let me beseech you. I would go on my knees to you, Oglethorpe, were they not already frozen. I beg of you do not doo—"

Here even the words froze on the water

ghost's lips and the clock struck one. There was a momentary tremor throughout the ice-bound form, and the moon, coming out from behind a cloud, shone down on the rigid figure of a beautiful woman sculptured in clear, transparent ice. There stood the ghost of Harrowby Hall, conquered by the cold, a prisoner for all time.

The heir of Harrowby had won at last, and to-day in a large storage house in London stands the frigid form of one who will never again flood the house of Oglethorpe with woe and sea-water.

As for the heir of Harrowby, his success in coping with a ghost has made him famous, a fame that still lingers about him, although his victory took place some twenty years ago; and so far from being unpopular with the fair sex, as he was when we first knew him, he has not only been married twice, but is to lead a third bride to the altar before the year is out.

THE SPECTRE COOK OF BAN GLETOP

I

FOR the purposes of this bit of history, Bangletop Hall stands upon a grassy knoll on the left bank of the River Dee, about eighteen miles from the quaint old city of Chester. It does not in reality stand there, nor has it ever done so, but consideration for the interests of the living compels me to conceal its exact location, and so to befog the public as to its whereabouts that its identity may never be revealed to its disadvantage. It is a rentable property, and were it known that it has had a mystery connected with it of so deep, dark, and eerie a nature as that about to be related, I fear that its usefulness, save as an accessory to romance, would be seriously

impaired, and that as an investment it
would become practically worthless.

The hall is a fair specimen of the architecture which prevailed at the time of Edward the Confessor ; that is to say, the main
portion of the structure, erected in Edward's
time by the first Baron Bangletop, has that
square, substantial, stony aspect which to
the eye versed in architecture identifies it at
once as a product of that enlightened era.
Later owners, the successive Barons Bangletop, have added to its original dimensions,
putting Queen Anne wings here, Elizabethan ells there, and an Italian - Renaissance
façade on the river front. A Wisconsin
water tower, connected with the main build-
ing by a low Gothic alleyway, stands to the
south ; while toward the east is a Greek
chapel, used by the present occupant as a
store-room for his wife's trunks, she having
lately returned from Paris with a wardrobe
calculated to last through the first half of
the coming London season. Altogether
Bangletop Hall is an impressive structure,
and at first sight gives rise to various emotions in the æsthetic breast ; some cavil,

others admire.   One leading architect of Berlin travelled all the way from his German home to Bangletop Hall to show that famous structure to his son, a student in the profession which his father adorned ; to whom he is said to have observed that, architecturally, Bangletop Hall was "cosmopolitan and omniperiodic, and therefore a liberal education to all who should come to study and master its details."   In short, Bangletop Hall was an object - lesson to young architects, and showed them at a glance that which they should ever strive to avoid.

Strange to say, for quite two centuries had Bangletop Hall remained without a tenant, and for nearly seventy-five years it had been in the market for rent, the barons, father and son, for many generations having found it impossible to dwell within its walls, and for a very good reason : no cook could ever be induced to live at Bangletop for a longer period than two weeks.   Why the queens of the kitchen invariably took what is commonly known as French leave no occupant could ever learn, because, male or female, the departed domestics never returned to tell, and even had they done so, the pride of the Bangletops would not have permitted them to listen to the explanation. The Bangletop escutcheon was clear of blots, no suspicion even of a conversational blemish appearing thereon, and it was always a matter of extreme satisfaction to the family that no one of its scions since the title was created had ever been known to speak directly to any one of lesser rank than himself, communication with inferiors being always had through the medium of a private secretary, himself a baron, or better, in reduced circumstances.

The first cook to leave Bangletop under circumstances of a Gallic nature — that is, without known cause, wages, or luggage— had been employed by Fitzherbert Alexander, seventeenth Baron of Bangletop, through Charles Mortimor de Herbert, Baron Peddlington, formerly of Peddlington Manor at Dunwoodie-on-the-Hike, his private secretary, a handsome old gentleman of sixty-five, who had been deprived of his estates by the crown in 1629 because he was sus-

pected of having inspired a comic broadside
published in those troublous days, and di-
rected against Charles the First, which had
set all London in a roar.

This broadside, one of very few which are
not preserved in the British Museum—and
a greater.tribute to its rarity could not be
devised—was called, "A Good Suggestion
as to ye Proper Use of ye Chinne Whisker,"
and consisted of a few lines of doggerel
printed beneath a caricature of the king,
with the crown hanging from his goatee,
reading as follows :

"*Ye King doth sporte a gallous grey goatee*
  Uponne ye chinne, where every one may see.
  And since ye Monarch's head's too small to holde
  With comfort to himselfe ye crowne of gold,
  Why not enwax and hooke ye goatee rare,
  And lette ye British crown hang down from
     there ?"

Whether or no the Baron of Peddlington
was guilty of this traitorous effusion no one,
not even the king, could ever really make
up his mind. The charge was never fully
proven, nor was De Herbert ever able to

A DEPARTING COOK

refute it successfully, although he made frantic efforts to do so. The king, eminently just in such matters, gave the baron the benefit of the doubt, and inflicted only half the penalty prescribed, confiscating his estates, and letting him keep his head and liberty. De Herbert's family begged the crown to reverse the sentence, permitting them to keep the estates, the king taking their uncle's head in lieu thereof, he being unmarried and having no children who would mourn his loss. But Charles was poor rather than vindictive at this period, and preferring to adopt the other course, turned a deaf ear to the petitioners. This was probably one of the earliest factors in the decadence of literature as a pastime for men of high station.

De Herbert would have starved had it not been for his old friend Baron Bangletop, who offered him the post of private secretary, lately made vacant by the death of the Duke of Algeria, who had been the incumbent of that office for ten years, and in a short time the Baron of Peddlington was in full charge of the domestic arrange-

ments of his friend.   It was far from easy,
the work that devolved upon him.   He was
a proud, haughty man, used to luxury of
every sort, to whom contact with those who
serve was truly distasteful; to whom the
necessity of himself serving was most gall-
ing; but he had the manliness to face the
hardships Fate had put upon him, particularly when he realized that Baron Bangletop's attitude towards servants was such
that he could with impunity impose on the
latter seven indignities for every one that
was imposed on him.   Misery loves company, particularly when she is herself the
hostess, and can give generously of her
stores to others.

Desiring to retrieve his fallen fortunes,
the Baron of Peddlington offered large
salaries to those whom he employed to
serve in the Bangletop menage, and on pay-
day, through an ingenious system of fines,
managed to retain almost seventy-five per
cent. of the funds for his own use.   Of this
Baron Bangletop, of course, could know
nothing.   He was aware that under De
Herbert the running expenses of his house-

hold were nearly twice what they had been under the dusky Duke of Algeria; but he also observed that repairs to the property, for which the late duke had annually paid out several thousands of pounds sterling, with very little to show for it, now cost him as many hundreds with no fewer tangible results. So he winked his eye—the only unaristocratic habit he had, by-the-way— and said nothing. The revenue was large enough, he had been known to say, to support himself and all his relatives in state, with enough left over to satisfy even Ali Baba and the forty thieves.

Had he foreseen the results of his complacency in financial matters, I doubt if he would have persisted therein.

For some ten years under De Herbert's management everything went smoothly and expensively for the Bangletop Hall people, and then there came a change. The Baron Bangletop rang for his breakfast one morning, and his breakfast was not. The cook had disappeared. Whither or why she had gone, the private secretary professed to be unable to say. That she could easily be

replaced, he was certain. Equally certain
was it that Baron Bangletop stormed and
raved for two hours, ate a cold breakfast—a
thing he never had been known to do before—and then departed for London to dine
at the club until Peddlington had secured a
successor to the departed cook, which the
private secretary succeeded in doing within
three days. The baron was informed of
his manager's success, and at the end of a
week returned to Bangletop Hall, arriving
there late on a Saturday night, hungry as a
bear, and not too amiable, the king having
negotiated a forcible loan with him during
his sojourn in the metropolis.

"Welcome to Bangletop, Baron," said De
Herbert, uneasily, as his employer alighted
from his coach.

"Blast your welcome, and serve the dinner," returned the baron, with a somewhat
ill grace.

At this the private secretary seemed
much embarrassed. "Ahem!" he said.
"I'll be very glad to have the dinner
served, my dear Baron; but the fact is
I — er — I have been unable to provide

anything but canned lobster and apples."

"What, in the name of Chaucer, does
this mean?" roared Bangletop, who was a
great admirer of the father of English poetry; chiefly because, as he was wont to say,
Chaucer showed that a bad speller could
be a great man, which was a condition of
affairs exactly suited to his mind, since in
the science of orthography he was weak,
like most of the aristocrats of his day. "I
thought you sent me word you had a cook?"

"Yes, Baron, I did; but the fact of the
matter is, sir, she left us last night, or, rather, early this morning."

"Another one of your beautiful Parisian
exits, I presume?" sneered the baron, tapping the floor angrily with his toe.

"Well, yes, somewhat so; only she got
her money first."

"Money!" shrieked the baron. "Money! Why in Liverpool did she get her
money? What did we owe her money for?
Rent?"

"No, Baron; for services. She cooked
three dinners."

" Well, you'll pay the bill out of your per-
quisites, that's all.   She's done no cooking
for me, and she gets no pay from me.   Why
do you think she left?"

" She said—"

" Never mind what she said, sir," cried
Bangletop, cutting De Herbert short.
" When I am interested in the table-talk of
cooks, I'll let you know.   What I wish to
hear is what do *you* think was the cause of
her leaving?"

" I have no opinion on the subject," replied the private secretary, with becoming
dignity.   " I only know that at four o'clock
this morning she knocked at my door, and
demanded her wages for four days, and
vowed she'd stay no longer in the house."

" And why, pray, did you not inform me
of the fact, instead of having me travel
away down here from London?" queried
Bangletop.

" You forget, Baron," replied De Herbert, with a deprecatory gesture—" you forget that there is no system of telegraphy by
which you could be reached.   I may be
poor, sir, but I'm just as much of a baron

as you are, and I will take the liberty of saying right here, in what would be the shadow of your beard, if you had one, sir, that a man who insists on receiving cable messages when no such things exist is rather rushing business."

"Pardon my haste, Peddlington, old chap," returned the baron, softening. "You are quite right. My desire was unreasonable; but I swear to you, by all my ancestral Bangletops, that I am hungry as a pit full of bears, and if there's one thing I can't eat, it is lobster and apples. Can't you scare up a snack of bread and cheese and a little cold larded fillet? If you'll supply the fillet, I'll provide the cold."

At this sally the Baron of Peddlington laughed and the quarrel was over. But none the less the master of Bangletop went to bed hungry; nor could he do any better in the morning at breakfast-time. The butler had not been trained to cook, and the coachman's art had once been tried on a boiled egg, which no one had been able to open, much less eat, and as it was the parlor-maid's Sunday off, there was abso-

lutely no one in the house who could prepare a meal.   The Baron of Bangletop had
a sort of sneaking notion that if there were
nobody around he could have managed the
spit or gridiron himself; but, of course, in
view of his position, he could not make the
attempt.   And so he once more returned to
London, and vowed never to set his foot
within the walls of Bangletop Hall again
until his ancestral home was provided with
a cook " copper-fastened and riveted to her
position."

And Bangletop Hall from that time was
as a place deserted.   The baron never returned, because he could not return without
violating his oath; for De Herbert was not
able to obtain a cook for the Bangletop
cuisine who would stay, nor was any one
able to discover why.   Cook after cook came,
stayed a day, a week, and one or two held
on for two weeks, but never longer.   Their
course was invariably the same—they would
leave without notice; nor could any induce-
ment be offered which would persuade them
to remain.   The Baron of Peddlington became, first round-shouldered, then deaf, and

PAY-DAY

then insane in his search for a permanent
cook, landing finally in an asylum, where
he died, four years after the demise of his
employer in London, of softening of the
brain.   His last words were, " Why did you
leave your last place ?"

And so time went on.   Barons of Bangletop were born, educated, and died.   Dynas-
ties rose and fell, but Bangletop Hall remained uninhabited, although it was not
until 1799 that the family gave up all hopes
of being able to use their ancestral home.
Tremendous alterations, as I have already
hinted, were made.   The drainage was carefully inspected, and a special apartment
connected with the kitchen, finished in hardwood, handsomely decorated, and hung with
rich tapestries, was provided for the cook,
in the vain hope that she might be induced
permanently to occupy her position.   The
Queen Anne wing and Elizabethan ell were
constructed, the latter to provide bowling-
alleys and smoking-rooms for the probable
cousins of possible culinary queens, and
many there were who accepted the office
with alacrity, throwing it up with still greater

alacrity before the usual fortnight passed.
Then the Bangletops saw clearly that it was
impossible for them to live there, and mov-
ing away, the house was announced to be
"for rent, with all modern improvements,
conveniently located, spacious grounds, especially adapted to the use of those who do
their own cooking." The last clause of the
announcement puzzled a great many people,
who went to see the mansion for no other
reason than to ascertain just what the announcement meant, and the line, which was
inserted in a pure spirit of facetious bravado,
was probably the cause of the mansion's
quickly renting, as hardly a month had
passed before it was leased for one year by
a retired London brewer, whose wife's curiosity had been so excited by the strange
wording of the advertisement that she travelled out to Bangletop to gratify it, fell in
love with the place, and insisted upon her
husband's taking it for a season. The luck
of the brewer and his wife was no better
than that of the Bangletops. Their cooks
—and they had fourteen during their stay
there—fled after an average service of four

days apiece, and later the tenants themselves were forced to give up and return to
London, where they told their friends that
the "'all was 'aunted," which might have
filled the Bangletops with concern had they
heard of it. They did not hear of it, however, for they and their friends did not know
the brewer and the brewer's friends, and as
for complaining to the Bangletop agent in
the matter, the worthy beer-maker thought
he would better not do that, because he had
hopes of being knighted some day, and he
did not wish to antagonize so illustrious a
family as the Bangletops by running down
their famous hall — an antagonism which
might materially affect the chances of himself and his good wife when they came to
knock at the doors of London society. The
lease was allowed to run its course, the rent
was paid when due, and at the end of the
stipulated term Bangletop Hall was once
more on the lists as for rent.

II

For fourscore years and ten did the same hard fortune pursue the owners of Bangletop.   Additions to the property were made immediately upon request of possible lessees. The Greek chapel was constructed in 1868 at the mere suggestion of a Hellenic prince, who came to England to write a history of the American rebellion, finding the information in back files of British newspapers exactly suited to the purposes of picturesque narrative, and no more misleading than most home-made history.   Bangletop was retired, "far from the gadding crowd," as the prince put it, and therefore just the place in which a historian of the romantic school might produce his *magnum opus* without disturbance ; the only objection being that there was no place whither the eminently Christian sojourner could go to worship according to his faith, he being a communicant in the Greek Church.   This defect Baron Bangletop immediately remedied by erecting and endowing the chapel ;

and his youngest son, having been found too delicate morally for the army, was appointed to the living and placed in charge of the chapel, having first embraced with considerable ardor the faith upon which the soul of the princely tenant was wont to feed. All of these improvements—chapel, priest, the latter's change of faith, and all— the Bangletop agent put at the exceedingly low sum of forty-two guineas per annum and board for the priest; an offer which the prince at once accepted, stipulating, however, that the lease should be terminable at any time he or his landlord should see fit. Against this the agent fought nobly, but without avail. The prince had heard rumors about the cooks of Bangletop, and he was wary. Finally the stipulation was accepted by the baron, with what result the reader need hardly be told. The prince stayed two weeks, listened to one sermon in classic university Greek by the youthful Bangletop, was deserted by his cook, and moved away.

After the departure of the prince the estate was neglected for nearly twenty-two

years, the owner having made up his mind
that the case was hopeless.   At the end of
that period there came from the United
States a wealthy shoemaker, Hankinson J.
Terwilliger by name, chief owner of the Terwilliger Three-dollar Shoe Company (Limited), of Soleton, Massachusetts, and to him
was leased Bangletop Hall, with all its rights
and appurtenances, for a term of five years.
Mr. Terwilliger was the first applicant for
the hall as a dwelling to whom the agent, at
the instance of the baron, spoke in a spirit
of absolute candor.   The baron was well on
in years, and he did not feel like getting into
trouble with a Yankee, so he said, at his
time of life.   The hall had been a thorn in
his flesh all his days, and he didn't care if
it was never occupied, and therefore he
wished nothing concealed from a prospec-
tive tenant.   It was the agent's candor more
than anything else that induced Mr. Terwilliger to close with him for the term of five
years.   He suspected that the Bangletops
did not want him for a tenant, and from the
moment that notion entered his head, he
was resolved that he would be a tenant.

"I'm as good a man as any baron that ever lived," he said; "and if it pleases Hankinson J. Terwilliger to live in a baronial hall, a baronial hall is where Hankinson J. Terwilliger puts up."

"We certainly have none of the feeling which your words seem to attribute to us, my dear sir," the agent had answered. "Baron Bangletop would feel highly honored to have so distinguished a sojourner in England as yourself occupy his estate, but he does not wish you to take it without fully understanding the circumstances. Desirable as Bangletop Hall is, it seems fated to be unoccupied because it is thought to be haunted, or something of that sort, the effect of which is to drive away cooks, and without cooks life is hardly an ideal."

Mr. Terwilliger laughed. "Ghosts and me are not afraid of each other," he said. "'Let 'em haunt,' I say; and as for cooks, Mrs. H. J. T. hasn't had a liberal education for nothing. We could live if all the cooks in creation were to go off in a whiff. We have daughters too, we have. Good smart American girls, who can adorn a palace or grace a hut on demand, not afraid of poverty, and able to take care of good round dollars. They can play the piano all the morning and cook dinner all the afternoon if they're called on to do it; so your difficulties ain't my difficulties. I'll take the hall at your figures; term, five years; and if the baron 'll come down and spend a month with us at any time, I don't care when, we'll show him what a big lap Luxury can get up when she tries."

And so it happened. The New York papers announced that Hankinson J. Terwilliger, Mrs. Terwilliger, the Misses Terwilliger, and Master Hankinson J. Terwilliger, Jun., of Soleton, Massachusetts, had plunged into the dizzy whirl of English society, and that the sole of the three-dollar shoe now trod the baronial halls of the Bangletops. Later it was announced that the Misses Terwilliger, of Bangletop Hall, had been presented to the queen; that the Terwilligers had entertained the Prince of Wales at Bangletop; in fact, the Terwilligers became an important factor in the letters of all foreign correspondents of American pa-

pers, for the president of the Terwilliger
Three - dollar Shoe Company, of Soleton,
Massachusetts (Limited), was now in full
possession of the historic mansion, and was
living up to his surroundings.

For a time everything was plain sailing
for the Americans at Bangletop. The dire
forebodings of the agent did not seem to be
fulfilled, and Mr. Terwilliger was beginning
to feel aggrieved. He had hired a house
with a ghost, and he wanted the use of it;
but when he reflected upon the consequences
below stairs, he held his peace. He was not
so sure, after he had stayed at Bangletop
awhile, and had had his daughters presented
to the queen, that he could be so independent of cooks as he had at first supposed.
Several times he had hinted rather broadly
that some of the old New England home-
made flap-jacks would be most pleasing to
his palate; but since the prince had spent
an afternoon on the lawn of Bangletop, the
young ladies seemed deeply pained at the
mere mention of their accomplishments in
the line of griddles and batter; nor could
Mrs. Terwilliger, after having tasted the

joys of aristocratic life, bring herself to don
the apron which so became her portly person in the early American days, and prepare
for her lord and master one of those de-
licious platters of poached eggs and breakfast bacon, the mere memory of which made
his mouth water.   In short, palatial surroundings had too obviously destroyed in
his wife and daughters all that capacity for
happiness in a hovel of which Mr. Terwilliger had been so proud, and concerning
which he had so eloquently spoken to Baron
Bangletop's agent, and he now found himself in the position of Damocles.   The hall
was leased for a term, entertainment had
been provided for the county with lavish
hand ; but success was dependent entirely
upon his ability to keep a cook, his family
having departed from their republican prin-
ciples, and the history of the house was
dead against a successful issue.   So he decided that, after all, it was better that the
ghost should be allowed to remain quies-
cent, and he uttered no word of complaint.

It was just as well, too, that Mr. Terwilliger held his peace, and refrained from ad-

dressing a complaining missive to the agent
of Bangletop Hall; for before a message of
that nature could have reached the person
addressed, its contents would have been
misleading, for at a quarter after midnight
on the morning of the date set for the first
of a series of grand banquets to the county
folk, there came from the kitchen of Bangletop Hall a quick succession of shrieks that
sent the three Misses Terwilliger into hysterics, and caused Hankinson J. Terwilliger's sole remaining lock to stand erect.
Mrs. Terwilliger did not hear the shrieks,
owing to a lately acquired habit of hearing nothing that proceeded from below
stairs.

The first impulse of Terwilliger *père* was
to dive down under the bedclothes, and endeavor to drown the fearful sound by his
own labored breathing, but he never yield-
ed to first impulses. So he awaited the
second, which came simultaneously with a
second series of shrieks and a cry for help
in the unmistakable voice of the cook; a
lady, by-the-way, who had followed the Terwilliger fortunes ever since the Terwilligers

began to have fortunes, and whose first capacity in the family had been the dual one
of mistress of the kitchen and confidante of
madame. The second impulse was to arise
in his might, put on a stout pair of the Terwilliger three-dollar brogans—the strongest
shoe made, having been especially devised
for the British Infantry in the Soudan—and
garments suitable to the occasion, namely, a
mackintosh and pair of broadcloth trousers,
and go to the rescue of the distressed domestic. This Hankinson J. Terwilliger at
once proceeded to do, arming himself with
a pair of horse-pistols, murmuring on the
way below a soft prayer, the only one he
knew, and which, with singular inappropri-
ateness on this occasion, began with the
words, " Now I lay me down to sleep."

"What's the matter, Judson?" queried
Mrs. Terwilliger, drowsily, as she opened
her eyes and saw her husband preparing for
the fray.

She no longer called him Hankinson, not
because she did not think it a good name,
nor was it less euphonious to her ear than
Judson, but Judson was Mr. Terwilliger's

TERWILLIGER TO THE RESCUE

middle name, and middle names were quite
the thing, she had observed, in the best circles.   It was doubtless due to this discovery
that her visiting cards had been engraved
to read " Mrs. H. Judson-Terwilliger," the
hyphen presumably being a typographical
error, for which the engraver was responsible.

" Matter enough," growled Hankinson. " I
have reason to believe that that jackass of
a ghost is on duty to-night."

At the word ghost a pseudo-aristocratic
shriek pervaded the atmosphere, and Mrs.
Terwilliger, forgetting her social position
for a moment, groaned " Oh, Hank !" and
swooned away.   And then the president of
the Terwilliger Three-dollar Shoe Company
of Soleton, Massachusetts (Limited), de-
scended to the kitchen.

Across the sill of the kitchen door lay the
culinary treasure whose lobster croquettes
the Prince of Wales had likened unto a
dream of Lucullus.   Within the kitchen
were signs of disorder.   Chairs were upset ;
the table was lying flat on its back, with its
four legs held rigidly up in the air ; the

kitchen library, consisting of a copy of *Marie Antoinette's Dream-Book;* a yellow - covered novel bearing the title *Little Lucy; or, The Kitchen-maid who Became a Marchioness;* and *Sixty Soups, by One who Knows,* lay strewn about the room, the *Dream-Book* sadly torn, and *Little Lucy* disfigured forever with batter.   Even to the unpractised eye it was evident that something had happened, and Mr. Terwilliger felt a cold chill mounting his spine three sections at a time.   Whether it was the chill or his concern for the prostrate cook that was responsible or not I cannot say, but for some cause or other Mr. Terwilliger immediately got down on his knees, in which position he gazed fearfully about him for a few minutes, and then timidly remarked, "Cook!"

There was no answer.

"Mary, I say.   Cook," he whispered, "what the deuce is the meaning of all this?"

A low moan was all that came from the cook, nor would Hankinson have listened to more had there been more to hear, for simultaneously with the moan he became uncomfortably conscious of a presence.   In

trying to describe it afterwards, Hankinson
said that at first he thought a cold draught
from a dank cavern filled with a million
eels, and a rattlesnake or two thrown in for
luck, was blowing over him, and he avowed
that it was anything but pleasant; and then
it seemed to change into a mist drawn
largely from a stagnant pool in a malarial
country, floating through which were great
quantities of finely chopped sea-weed, wet
hair, and an indescribable atmosphere of
something the chief quality of which was a
sort of stale clamminess that was awful in
its intensity.

"I'm glad," Mr. Terwilliger murmured to
himself, "that I ain't one of those delicately
reared nobles. If I had anything less than
a right-down regular republican constitution
I'd die of fright."

And then his natural grit came to his
rescue, and it was well it did, for the presence had assumed shape, and now sat on
the window-ledge in the form of a hag, glar-
ing at him from out of the depths of her
unfathomable eyes, in which, despite their
deadly greenness, there lurked a tinge of red

caused by small specks of that hue semi-occasionally seen floating across her dilated pupils.

"You are the Bangletop ghost, I presume?" said Terwilliger, rising and standing near the fire to thaw out his system.

The spectre made no reply, but pointed to the door.

"Yes," Terwilliger said, as if answering a question. "That's the way out, madame. It's a beautiful exit, too. Just try it."

"H'I knows the wi out," returned the spectre, rising and approaching the tenant of Bangletop, whose solitary lock also rose, being too polite to remain seated while the ghost walked. "H'I also knows the wi in, 'Ankinson Judson Terwilliger."

"That's very evident, madame, and between you and me I wish you didn't," returned Hankinson, somewhat relieved to hear the ghost talk, even if her voice did sound like the roar of a conch-shell with a bad case of grip. "I may say to you that, aside from a certain uncanny satisfaction which I feel at being permitted for the first time in my life to gaze upon the linaments

THE PRESENCE HAD ASSUMED SHAPE

of a real live misty musty spook, I regard your coming here as an invasion of the sacred rights of privacy which is, as you might say, 'hinexcusable.'"

"Hinvaision?" retorted the ghost, snapping her fingers in his face with such effect that his chin dropped until Terwilliger began to fear it might never resume its normal position. "Hinvaision? H'I'd like to know 'oo's the hinvaider. H'I've occupied hese 'ere 'alls for hover two 'undred years."

"Then it's time you moved, unless perchance you are the ghost of a mediæval porker," Hankinson said, his calmness returning now that he had succeeded in plastering his iron-gray lock across the top of his otherwise bald head. "Of course, if you are a spook of that kind you want the earth, and maybe you'll get it."

"H'I'm no porker," returned the spectre. "H'I'm simply the shide of a poor abused cook which is hafter revenge."

"Ah!" ejaculated Terwilliger, raising his eyebrows, "this is getting interesting. You're a spook with a grievance, eh? Against me? I've never wronged a ghost that I know of."

"No, h'I've no 'ard feelinks against you, sir," answered the ghost. "Hin fact h'I don't know nothink about you. My trouble's with them Baingletops, and h'I'm a-pursuin' of 'em. H'I've cut 'em out of two 'undred years of rent 'ere. They might better 'ave pide me me waiges hin full."

"Oho!" cried Terwilliger; "it's a question of wages, is it? The Bangletops were hard up?"

"'Ard up? The Baingletops?" laughed the ghost. "When they gets 'ard up the Baink o' Hengland will be in all the sixty soups mentioned in that there book."

"You seem to be up in the vernacular," returned Terwilliger, with a smile. "I'll bet you are an old fraud of a modern ghost."

Here he discharged all six chambers of his pistol into the body of the spectre.

"No taikers," retorted the ghost, as the bullets whistled through her chest, and struck deep into the wall on the other side of the kitchen. "That's a noisy gun you've got, but you carn't ly a ghost with co'd lead hany more than you can ly a corner-stone

"'NO TAKERS,' RETORTED THE GHOST"

with a chicken. H'I'm 'ere to sty until I
gets me waiges."

"What was the amount of your wages
due at the time of your discharge?" asked
Hankinson.

"H'I was gettin' ten pounds a month,"
returned the spectre.

"Geewhittaker!" cried Terwilliger, "you
must have been an all-fired fine cook."

"H'I was," assented the ghost, with a
proud smile. "H'I cooked a boar's 'ead
for 'is Royal 'Ighness King Charles when
'e visited Baingletop 'All as which was the
finest 'e hever taisted, so 'e said, hand 'e'd
'ave knighted me hon the spot honly me
sex wasn't suited to the title. 'You carn't
make a knight out of a woman,' says the
king, ' but give 'er my compliments, and tell
'er 'er monarch says as 'ow she's a cook as
is too good for 'er staition.'"

"That was very nice," said Terwilliger.
"No one could have desired a higher rec-
ommendation than that."

"My words hexackly when the baron's
privit secretary told me two dys laiter as
'ow the baron's heggs wasn't done proper,"

said the ghost. "H'I says to 'im, says I :
'The baron's heggs be blowed. My monarch's hopinion is worth two of any ten
barons's livin', and Mister Baingletop,' (h'I
allus called 'im mister when 'e was ugly,) ' can
get 'is heggs cooked helsewhere if 'e don't
like the wy h'I boils 'em.' Hand what do
you suppose the secretary said then ?"

"I give it up," replied Terwilliger.
"What ?"

"'E said as 'ow h'I 'ad the big 'ead."

"How disgusting of him !" murmured
Terwilliger. "That was simply low."

"Hand then 'e accuged me of bein' him-
pudent."

"No !"

"'E did, hindeed ; hand then 'e discharged me without me waiges. Hof course
h'I wouldn't sty after that ; but h'I says to
'im, ' Hif I don't get me py, h'I'll 'aunt
this place from the dy of me death ;' hand
'e says, ''Aunt awy.'"

"And you have kept your word."

"H'I 'ave that !   H'I've made it 'ot for
'em, too."

"Well, now, look here," said Terwilliger,

"I'll tell you what I'll do. I'll pay you your wages if you'll go back to Spookland and mind your own business. Ten pounds isn't much when three-dollar shoes cost fifteen cents a pair and sell like hot waffles. Is it a bargain?"

"H'I was sent off with three months' money owin' me," said the ghost.

"Well, call it thirty pounds, then," replied Terwilliger.

"With hinterest — compound hinterest at six per cent.—for two 'undred and thirty years," said the ghost.

"Phew!" whistled Terwilliger. "Have you any idea how much money that is?"

"Certingly," replied the ghost. "Hit's just 63,609,609 pounds 6 shillings 4½ pence. When h'I gets that, h'I flies; huntil I gets it h'I stys 'ere an' I 'aunts."

"Say," said Terwilliger, "haven't you been chumming with an Italian ghost named Shylock over on the other shore?"

"Shylock!" said the ghost. "No, h'I've never 'eard the naime. Perhaps 'e's stoppin' at the hother place."

"Very likely," said Terwilliger. "He is

an eminent saint alongside of you.   But I say now, Mrs. Spook, or whatever your name is, this is rubbing it in, to try to collect as much money as that, particularly from me, who wasn't to blame in any way, and on whom you haven't the spook of a claim."

" H'I'm very sorry for you, Mr. Terwilliger," said the ghost.   " But my vow must be kept sacrid."

" But why don't you come down on the Bangletops up in London, and squeeze it out of them?"

" H'I carn't.   H'I'm bound to 'aunt this 'all, an' that's hall there is about it.   H'I carn't find a better wy to ly them Baingletops low than by attachin' of their hincome, hand the rent of this 'all is the honly bit of hincome within my reach."

" But I've leased the place for five years," said Terwilliger, in despair ; " and I've paid the rent in advance."

" Carn't 'elp it," returned the ghost.   " Hif you did that, hit's your own fault."

" I wouldn't have done it, except to advertise my shoe business," said Terwilliger, ruefully. "The items in the papers at home that arise from my occupancy of this house, together with the social cinch it gives me, are worth the money; but I'm hanged if it's worth my while to pay back salaries to every grasping apparition that chooses to rise up out of the moat and dip his or her clammy hand into my surplus. The shoe trade is a blooming big thing, but the profits aren't big enough to divide with tramp ghosts."

" Your tone is very 'aughty, 'Ankinson J. Terwilliger, but it don't haffeck me. H'I don't care 'oo pys the money, an' h'I 'aven't got you into this scripe. You've done that yourself. Hon the other 'and, sir, h'I've showed you 'ow to get out of it."

"Well, perhaps you're right," returned Hankinson. " I can't say I blame you for not perjuring yourself, particularly since you've been dead long enough to have discovered what the probable consequences would be. But I do wish there was some other way out of it. *I* couldn't pay you all that money without losing a controlling interest in the shoe company, and that's hardly worth my while, now is it?"

"No, Mr. Terwilliger; hit is not."

"I have a scheme," said Hankinson, after a moment or two of deep thought. "Why don't you go back to the spirit world and expose the Bangletops there? They have spooks, haven't they?"

"Yes," replied the ghost, sadly. "But the spirit world his as bad as this 'ere. The spook of a cook carn't reach the spook of a baron there hany more than a scullery-maid can reach a markis 'ere. H'I tried that when the baron died and came over to the hother world, but 'e 'ad 'is spook flunkies on 'and to tell me 'e was hout drivin' with the ghost of William the Conqueror and the shide of Solomon. H'I knew 'e wasn't, but what could h'I do?"

"It was a mean game of bluff," said Terwilliger. "I suppose, though, if you were the shade of a duchess, you could simply knock Bangletop silly?"

"Yes, and the Baron of Peddlington too. 'E was the private secretary as said h'I 'ad the big 'ead."

"H'm!" said Terwilliger, meditatively. "Would you—er—would you consent to retire from this haunting business of yours, and give me a receipt for that bill for wages, interest and all, if I had you made over into the spook of a duchess?   Revenge is sweet, you know, and there are some revenges that are simply a thousand times more balmy than riches."

"Would h'I?" ejaculated the ghost, rising and looking at the clock.   "Would h'I?" she repeated.   "Well, rather.   If h'I could enter spook society as a duchess, you can wager a year's hincome them Bangletops wouldn't be hin it."

"Good!   I am glad to see that you are a spook of spirit.   If you had veins, I believe there 'd be sporting blood in them."

"Thainks," said the ghost, dryly.   "But 'ow can it hever be did?"

"Leave that to me," Terwilliger answered. "We'll call a truce for two weeks, at the end of which time you must come back here, and we'll settle on the final arrangements.   Keep your own counsel in the matter, and don't breathe a word about your intentions to anybody.   Above all, keep sober."

"H'I'm no cannibal," retorted the ghost.

"Who said you were?" asked Terwilliger.

"You intimated as much," said the ghost, with a smile. "You said as 'ow I must keep sober, and 'ow could I do hotherwise hunless I swallered some spirits?"

Terwilliger laughed. He thought it was a pretty good joke for a ghost—especially a cook's ghost—and then, having agreed on the hour of midnight one fortnight thence for the next meeting, they shook hands and parted.

"What was it, Hankinson?" asked Mrs. Terwilliger, as her husband crawled back into bed. "Burglars?"

"Not a burglar," returned Hankinson. "Nothing but a ghost—a poor, old, female ghost."

"Ghost!" cried Mrs. Terwilliger, trembling with fright. "In this house?"

"Yes, my dear. Haunted us by mistake, that's all. Belongs to another place entirely; got a little befogged, and came here without intending to, that's all. When she found out her mistake, she apologized, and left."

THEY SHOOK HANDS AND PARTED

"What did she have on?" asked Mrs. Terwilliger, with a sigh of relief.

But the president of the Three - dollar Shoe Company, of Soleton, Massachusetts (Limited), said nothing. He had dropped off into a profound slumber.

III

For the next two weeks Terwilliger lived in a state of preoccupation that worried his wife and daughters to a very considerable extent. They were afraid that something had happened, or was about to happen, in connection with the shoe corporation ; and this deprived them of sleep, particularly the elder Miss Terwilliger, who had danced four times at a recent ball with an impecunious young earl, whom she suspected of having intentions. Ariadne was in a state of grave apprehension, because she knew that much as the earl might love her, it would be difficult for them to marry on his income, which was literally too small to

keep the roof over his head in decent re-
pair.

But it was not business troubles that occupied every sleeping and waking thought
of Hankinson Judson Terwilliger.   His
mind was now set upon the hardest problem
it had ever had to cope with, that problem
being how to so ennoble the spectre cook
of Bangletop that she might outrank the
ancestors of his landlord in the other world
—the shady world, he called it.   The living
cook had been induced to remain partly by
threats and partly by promises of increased
pay ; the threats consisting largely of ex-
pressions of determination to leave her in
England, thousands of miles from her home
in Massachusetts, deserted and forlorn, the
poor woman being insufficiently provided
with funds to get back to America, and
holding in her veins a strain of Celtic blood
quite large enough to make the idea of remaining an outcast in England absolutely
intolerable to her.   At the end of seven
days Terwilliger was seemingly as far from
the solution of his problem as ever, and at
the grand fête given by himself and wife on

the afternoon of the seventh day of his
trial, to the Earl of Mugley, the one in
whom Ariadne was interested, he seemed
almost rude to his guests, which the latter
overlooked, taking it for the American way
of entertaining. It is very hard for a shoemaker to entertain earls, dukes, and the
plainest kind of every-day lords under ordinary circumstances; but when, in addition
to the duties of host, the maker of soles has
to think out a recipe for the making of an
aristocrat out of a deceased plebe, a polite
drawing - room manner is hardly to be expected. Mr. Terwilliger's manner remained
of the kind to be expected under the circumstances, neither better nor worse, until
the flunky at the door announced, in sten-
torian tones, "The Hearl of Mugley."

The "Hearl" of Mugley seemed to be
the open sesame to the door betwixt Terwilliger and success. Simultaneously with
the entrance of the earl the solution of his
problem flashed across the mind of the
master of Bangletop, and his affronting de-
meanor, his preoccupation and all disappeared in an instant. Indeed, so elegantly

enthusiastic was his reception of the earl
that Lady Maud Sniffles, on the other side
of the room, whispered in the ear of the
Hon. Miss Pottleton that Mugley's creditors were in luck; to which the Hon. Miss
Pottleton, whose smiles upon the nobleman
had been returned unopened, curved her
upper lip spitefully, and replied that they
were indeed, but she didn't envy Ariadne
that pompous little error of nature's, the
earl.

"Howdy do, Earl?" said Terwilliger.
"Glad to see you looking so well. How's
your mamma?"

"The countess is in her usual state of
health, Mr. Terwilliger," returned the earl.

"Ain't she coming this afternoon?"

"I really can't say," answered Mugley.
"I asked her if she was coming, and all she
did was to call for her salts. She's a little
given to fainting-spells, and the slightest
shock rather upsets her."

And then the earl turned on his heel and
sought out the fair Ariadne, while Terwilliger, excusing himself, left the assemblage,
and went directly to his private office in the

THE H'EARL OF MUGLEY

crypt of the Greek chapel. Arrived there, he seated himself at his desk and wrote the following formal card, which he put in an envelope and addressed to the Earl of Mugley:

"If the Earl of Mugley will call at the private office of Mr. H. Judson Terwilliger at once, he will not only greatly oblige Mr. H. Judson Terwilliger, but may also hear of something to his advantage."

The card written, Terwilliger summoned an attendant, ordered a quantity of liqueurs, whiskey, sherry, port, and lemon squash for two to be brought to the office, and then sent his communication to the earl.

Now the earl was a great stickler for etiquette, and he did not at all like the idea of one in his position waiting upon one of Mr. Terwilliger's rank, or lack of rank, and, at first thought, he was inclined to ignore the request of his host, but a combination of circumstances served to change his resolution. He so seldom heard anything to his advantage that, for mere novelty's sake, he thought he would do as he was asked; but the question of his dignity rose up again,

and shoving the note into his pocket he
tried to forget it.   After five minutes he
found he could not forget it, and putting his
hand into the pocket for the missive, meaning to give it a second reading, he drew out
another paper by mistake, which was, in
brief, a reminder from a firm of London
lawyers that he owed certain clients of
theirs a few thousands of pounds for the
clothing that had adorned his back for the
last two years, and stating that proceedings
would be begun if at the expiration of three
months the account was not paid in full.
The reminder settled it.   The Earl of Mugley graciously concluded to grant Mr. H.
Judson Terwilliger an audience in the private office under the Greek chapel.

"Sit down, Earl, and have a cream de
mint with me," said Terwilliger, as the earl,
four minutes later, entered the apartment.

" Thanks," returned the earl.   " Beautiful color that," he added, pleasantly, smacking his lips with satisfaction as the soft
green fluid disappeared from the glass into
his inner earl.

"Fine," said Terwilliger.   " Little unripe,

perhaps, but pleasant to the eye. I prefer
the hue of the Maraschino, myself. Just
taste that Maraschino, Earl. It's A1; thirty-
six dollars a case."

"You wanted to see me about some matter of interest to both of us, I believe, Mr.
Terwilliger," said the earl, declining the
proffered Maraschino.

"Well, yes," returned Terwilliger. "More
of interest to you, perhaps, than to me. The
fact is, Earl, I've taken quite a shine to you,
so much of a one in fact, that I've looked
you up at a commercial agency, and H. J.
Terwilliger never does that unless he's
mightily interested in a man."

"I—er—I hope you are not to be prejudiced against me," the earl said, uneasily,
"by—er—by what those cads of tradesmen
say about me."

"Not a bit," returned Terwilliger—"not
a bit. In fact, what I've discovered has
prejudiced me in your favor. You are just
the man I've been looking for for some
days. I've wanted a man with three A blood
and three Z finances for 'most a week now,
and from what I gather from Burke and

Bradstreet, you fill the bill. You owe pretty much everybody from your tailor to the collector of pew rents at your church, eh ?"

" I've been unfortunate in financial matters," returned the earl ; " but I have left the family name untarnished."

" So I believe, Earl. That's what I admire about you. Some men with your debts would be driven to drink or other pastimes of a more or less tarnishing nature, and I admire you for the admirable restraint you have put upon yourself. You owe, I am told, about twenty-seven thousand pounds."

" My secretary has the figures, I believe," said the earl, slightly bored.

" Well, we'll say thirty thousand in round figures. Now what hope have you of ever paying that sum off ?"

" None — unless I — er — well, unless I should be fortunate enough to secure a rich wife."

" Precisely ; that is exactly what I thought," rejoined Terwilliger. " Marriage is your only asset, and as yet that is hardly negotiable. Now I have called you here this afternoon to make a proposition to you. If

you will marry according to my wishes I
will give you an income of five thousand
pounds a year for the next five years."

"I don't quite understand you," the earl
replied, in a disappointed tone. It was evident that five thousand pounds per annum
was too small a figure for his tastes.

"I think I was quite plain," said Terwilliger, and he repeated his offer.

"I certainly admire the lady very much,"
said the earl; "but the settlement of income seems very small."

Terwilliger opened his eyes wide with astonishment. "Oh, you admire the lady,
eh?" he said. "Well, there is no account-
ing for tastes."

"You surprise me slightly," said the earl,
in response to this remark. "The lady is
certainly worthy of any man's admiration. She is refined, cultivated, beautiful,
and—"

"Ahem!" said Terwilliger. "May I ask,
my dear Earl, to whom you refer?"

"To Ariadne, of course. I thought your
course somewhat unusual, but we do not
pretend to comprehend you Americans over

here.   Your proposition is that I shall marry Ariadne ?"

I hesitate to place on record what Terwilliger said in answer to this statement.
It was forcible rather than polite, and the
earl from that moment adopted a new sim-
ile for degrees of profanity, substituting "to
swear like an American " for the old forms
having to do with pirates and troopers.
The string of expletives was about five
minutes in length, at the end of which
time Terwilliger managed to say :

" No such d—— proposition ever entered
my mind. I want you to marry a cold,
misty, musty spectre, nothing more or less,
and I'll tell you why."

And then he proceeded to tell the Earl of
Mugley all that he knew of the history of
Bangletop Hall, concluding with a narra-
tion of his experiences with the ghost cook.

" My rent here," he said, in conclusion,
" is five thousand pounds per annum. The
advertising I get out of the fact of my being here and swelling it with you nabobs is
worth twenty-five thousand pounds a year,
and I'm willing to pay, in good hard cash,

" ' TO ARIADNE, OF COURSE ' "

twenty per cent. of that amount rather than
be forced to give up. Now here's your
chance to get an income without an encum-
brance and stave off your creditors. Marry the spook, so that she can go back to the
spirit land a countess and make it hot for
the Bangletops, and don't be so allfired
proud. She'll be disappointed enough I
can tell you, when I inform her that an earl
was the best I could do, the promised duke
not being within reach. If she says earls
are drugs in the market, I won't be able to
deny it; and, after all, my lad, a good cook
is a greater blessing in this world than any
earl that ever lived, and a blamed sight
rarer."

"Your proposition is absolutely ridicu-
lous, Mr. Terwilliger," replied the earl.
"I'd look well marrying a draught from
a dark cavern, as you call it, now wouldn't
I? To say nothing of the impossibility of
a Mugley marrying a cook. I cannot entertain the proposition."

"You'll find you can't entertain anything
if you don't watch out," fumed Terwilliger,
in return.

" I'm not so sure about that," replied the
earl, haughtily, sipping his lemon squash.
" I fancy Miss Ariadne is not entirely in-
different to me."

" Well, you might just as well understand
on this 18th day of July, 18—, as any other
time, that my daughter Ariadne never becomes the Earless of Mugley," said Terwilliger, in a tone of exasperation.

" Not even when her father considers the
commercial value of such an alliance for his
daughter ?" retorted the earl, shaking his
finger in Terwilliger's face.   " Not even
when the President of the Three-dollar
Shoe Company, of Soleton, Massachusetts
(Limited), considers the advertising sure
to result from a marriage between his house
and that of Mugley, with presents from her
majesty the queen, the Duke of York acting as best man, and telegrams of congrat-
ulation from the crowned heads of Europe
pouring in at the rate of two an hour for
half as many hours as there are thrones ?"

Terwilliger turned pale.

The picture painted by the earl was ter-
ribly alluring.

He hesitated.

He was lost.

"Mugley," he whispered, hoarsely—
"Mugley, I have wronged you. I thought
you were a fortune-hunter. I see you love
her. Take her, my boy, and pass me the
brandy."

"Certainly, Mr. Terwilliger," replied the
earl, affably. "And then, if you've no objection, you may pass it back, and I'll join
you in a thimbleful myself."

And then the two men drank each other's health in silence, which was prolonged
for at least five minutes, during which time
the earl and his host both appeared to be
immersed in deep thought.

"Come," said Terwilliger at last. "Let
us go back to the drawing-room, or they'll
miss us, and, by-the-way, you might speak
of that little matter to Ariadne to-night.
It'll help the fall trade to have the engagement announced."

"I will, Mr. Terwilliger," returned the
earl, as they started to leave the room;
"but I say, father-in-law elect," he whispered, catching Terwilliger's coat sleeve and

drawing him back into the office for an instant, "you couldn't let me have five pounds
on account this evening, could you?"

Two minutes later Terwilliger and the
earl appeared in the drawing-room, the former looking haggard and worn, his eyes fe-
verishly bright, and his manner betraying
the presence of disturbing elements in his
nerve centres; the latter smiling more affably than was consistent with his title, and
jingling a number of gold coins in his pocket, which his intimate friend and old college
chum, Lord Dufferton, on the other side of
the room, marvelled at greatly, for he knew
well that upon the earl's arrival at Bangletop Hall an hour before his pockets were
as empty as a flunky's head.

IV

Terwilliger's time was almost up. The
hour for his interview with the spectre cook
of Bangletop was hardly forty-eight hours
distant, and he was wellnigh distracted. No

solution of the problem seemed possible
since the earl had so peremptorily declined
to fall in with his plan. He was glad the
earl had done so, for otherwise he would
have been denied the tremendous satisfaction which the consummation of an alliance
between his own and one of the oldest and
noblest houses of England was about to
give him, not to mention the commercial
phase of the situation, which had been so
potent a factor in bringing the engagement
about; for Ariadne had said yes to the earl
that same night, and the betrothal was shortly to be announced. It would have been
announced at once, only the earl felt that he
should break the news himself first to his
mother, the countess—an operation which
he dreaded, and for which he believed some
eight or ten weeks of time were necessary.

"What is the matter, Judson?" Mrs. Terwilliger asked finally, her husband was growing so careworn of aspect.

"Nothing, my dear, nothing."

"But there is something, Judson, and as
your wife I demand to know what it is.
Perhaps I can help you."

And then Mr. Terwilliger broke down, and told the whole story to Mrs. Terwilliger, omitting no detail, stopping only to bring that worthy lady to on the half-dozen or more occasions when her emotions were too strong for her nerves, causing her to swoon. When he had quite done, she looked him reproachfully in the eye, and said that if he had told her the truth instead of deceiving her on the night of the spectral visitation, he might have been spared all his trouble.

"For you know, Judson," she said, "I have made a study of the art of acquiring titles. Since I read the story of the girl who started in life as an innkeeper's daughter and died a duchess, by Elizabeth Harley Hicks, of Salem, and realized how one might be lowly born and yet rise to lofty heights, it has been my dearest wish that my girls might become noblewomen, and at times, Judson, I have even hoped that you might yet become a duke."

"Great Scott!" ejaculated Terwilliger. "That would be awful. Hankinson, Duke of Terwilliger! Why, Molly, I'd never be

" ' A DUKE'S A DUKE THE WORLD OVER ' "

able to hold up my head in shoe circles
with a name on me like that."

" Is there nothing in the world but shoes,
Judson ?" asked his wife, seriously.

" You'll find shoes are the foundation
upon which society stands," chuckled Terwilliger in return.

" You are never serious," returned Mrs.
Terwilliger ; " but now you must be. You
are coping with the supernatural. Now I
have discovered," continued the lady, " that
there are three methods by which titles are
acquired—birth, marriage, and purchase."

" You forget the fourth—achievement,"
suggested Terwilliger.

" Not these days, Judson. It used to be
so, but it is not so now. Now the spectre
hasn't birth, we can't get any living duke to
marry her, dead dukes are hard to find, so
there's nothing to do but to buy her a title."

" But where ?"

" In Italy. You can get 'em by the doz-
en. Every hand-organ grinder in America
grinds away in the hope of going back to
Italy and purchasing a title. Why can't
you do the same?"

"Me? Me grind a hand-organ in America?" cried Hankinson.

"No, no; purchase a dukedom."

"I don't want a dukedom; I want a duchessdom."

"That's all right. Buy the title, give it to the cook, and let her marry some spectre of her own rank; she can give him the title; and there you are!"

"Good scheme!" cried Terwilliger. "But I say, Molly, don't you think it would be better to get her to bring the spectre over here, and have me give him the title, and then let him marry her here?"

"No, I don't. If you give it to him first, the chances are he would go back on his bargain. He'd say that, being a duke, he couldn't marry a cook."

"You have a large mind, Molly," said Terwilliger.

"I know men!" snapped Mrs. Terwilliger.

And so it happened. Hankinson Judson Terwilliger applied by wire to the authorities in Rome for all right, title, and interest in one dukedom, free from encumbrances, irrevocable, and duly witnessed by the proper dignitaries of the Italian government, and at the second interview with the spectre cook of Bangletop, he was able to show her a cablegram received from the Eternal City stating that the papers would be sent upon receipt of the applicant's check for one hundred lire.

"'Ow much his that?" asked the ghost.

"One hundred lire?" returned Terwilliger, repeating the sum to gain time to think. He was himself surprised at the cheapness of the duchy, and he was afraid that if the ghost knew its real value she would decline to take it. "One hundred lire? Why, that's about 750,000 dollars — 150,000 pounds. They charge high for their titles," he added, blushing slightly.

"Pretty 'igh," returned the ghost. "But h'I carn't be a duke, ye know. 'Ow'll I manidge that?"

Hankinson explained his wife's scheme to the spectre.

"That's helegant," said she. "H'I've loved a butler o' the Bangletops for nigh hon to two 'undred years, but, some'ow or hother, he's kep' shy o' me. This 'll fix 'im.

But h'I say, Mr. Terwilliger, his one o' them Heyetalian dukes as good as a Henglish one ?"

" Every bit," said Terwilliger. " A duke's a duke the world over. Don't you know the lines of Burns, ' A duke's a duke for a' that'?"

" Never 'eard of 'im," replied the ghost.

" Well, you look him up when you get settled down at home. He was a smart man here, and, if his ghost does him justice, you'll be mighty glad to know him," Terwilliger answered.

And thus was Bangletop Hall delivered of its uncanny visitor. The ducal appointment, entitling its owner to call himself " Duke of Cavalcadi," was received in due time, and handed over to the curse of the kitchen, who immediately disappeared, and permanently, from the haunts that had known her for so long and so disadvantageously. Bangletop Hall is now the home of a happy family, to whom all are devoted, and from whose *ménage* no cook has ever been known to depart, save for natural causes, despite all that has gone before.

BACK TO THE SPIRIT VALE

Ariadne has become Countess of Mugley, and Mrs. Terwilliger is content with her Judson, whom, however, she occasionally calls Duke of Cavalcadi, claiming that he is the representative of that ancient and noble family on earth. As for Judson, he always smiles when his wife calls him Duke, but denies the titular impeachment, for he is on good terms with his landlord, whose admiration for his tenant's wholly unexpected ability to retain his cook causes him to regard him as a supernatural being, and therefore worthy of a Bangletop's regard.

"All of which," Terwilliger says to Mrs. Terwilliger, "might not be so, my dear, were I really the duke, for I honestly believe that if there is a feud of long standing anywhere in the universe, it is between the noble families of Bangletop and Cavalcadi over on the other shore."

THE SPECK ON THE LENS

"TALKING about inventions," said the oculist, as he very dexterously pocketed two of the pool balls, the handsome ringer, more familiarly known as the fifteen ball, and the white ball itself, thereby adding somewhat to the minus side of his string— "talking about inventions, I had a curious experience last August. It was an experience which was not only interesting from an inventive point of view, but it had likewise a moral, which will become more or less obvious as I unfold the story.

"You know I rented and occupied a place in Yonkers last summer. It was situated on the high lands to the north of the city, a little this side of Greystone, overlooking that magnificent stream, the Hudson, the ever-varying beauties of which so few of the residents along its banks really appreci-

ate.   It was a comfortable spot, with a few
trees about it, a decent-sized garden—large
enough to raise a tomato or two for a Sun-
day-night salad—and a lawn which was a
cure for sore eyes, its soft, sheeny surface
affording a most restful object upon which
to feast the tired optic.   I believe it was
that lawn that first attracted me as I drove
by the place with a patient I had in tow.
It was just after a heavy shower, and the
sun breaking through the clouds and lighting up the rain-soaked grass gave to it a
glistening golden greenness that to my eyes
was one of the most beautiful and soul-sat-
isfying bits of color I had seen in a long
time.   'Oh, for a summer of that!' I said to
myself, little thinking that the beginning of
a summer thereof *was* to fall to my lot before many days—for on May 1st I signed
papers which made me to all intents and
purposes proprietor of the place for the en-
suing six months.

"At one corner of the grounds stood, I
should say, a dozen apple-trees, the spread-
ing branches of which seemed to form a
roof for a sort of enchanted bower, in which,

you may be sure, I passed many of my leisure hours, swinging idly in a hammock, the
cool breezes from the Hudson, concerning
which so many people are sceptical, but
which nevertheless exist, bringing delight
to the ear and nostril as well as to the
'fevered brow,' which is so fashionable in
the neighborhood of New York in the summer, making the leaves rustle in a tuneful
sort of fashion, and laden heavily with the
sweet odors of many a garden close over
which they passed before they got to me."

"Put that in rhyme, doctor, and there's
your poem," said the lieutenant, as he made
a combination scratch involving every ball
on the table.

"I'll do it," said the doctor; "and then
I'll have it printed as Appendix J to the
third edition of my work on *Sixty Astigma-
tisms, and How to Acquire Them*. But to get
back to my story," he continued. "I was
lying there in my hammock one afternoon
trying to take a census of the butterflies in
sight, when I thought I heard some one
back of me call me by name. Instantly
the butterfly census was forgotten, and I

was on the alert; but—whether there was something the matter with my eyes or not, I do not know—despite all my alertness, there wasn't a soul in sight that I could see. Of course, I was slightly mystified at first, and then I attributed the interruption either to imagination or to some passer-by, whose voice, wafted on the breeze, might have reached my ears. I threw myself back into the hammock once more, and was just about dozing off to the lullaby sung by a bee to the accompaniment of the rustling leaves, when I again heard my name distinctly spoken.

" This time there was no mistake about it, for as I sprang to my feet and looked about, I saw coming towards me a man of unpleasantly cadaverous aspect, whose years, I should judge, were at least eighty in number. His beard was so long and scant that, to keep the breezes from blowing it about to his discomfort, he had tucked the ends of it into his vest pocket; his eyes, black as coals, were piercing as gimlets, their sharpness equalled by nothing that I had ever seen, excepting perhaps the point

of this same person's nose, which was long
and thin, suggesting a razor with a bowie
point; his slight body was clad in sombre
garb, and at first glance he appeared to me
so disquietingly like a visitor from the supernatural world that I shuddered; but when
he spoke, his voice was all gentleness, and
whatever of fear I had experienced was in a
moment dissipated.

"'You are Doctor Carey?' he said, in a
timid sort of fashion.

"'Yes,' I replied; 'I am.   What can I
do for you?'

"'The distinguished oculist?' he added,
as if not hearing my question.

"'Well, I'm a sort of notorious eye-doc-
tor,' I answered, my well-known modesty
preventing my entire acquiescence in his
manner of putting it.

"He smiled pleasantly as I said this, and
then drew out of his coat-tail pocket a small
tin box, which, until he opened it, I supposed contained a drinking-cup — one of
those folding tin cups.

"'Doctor Carey,' said he, sitting down in
the hammock which I had vacated, and toy-

ing with the tin box—a proceeding that was
so extraordinarily cool that it made me
shiver—'I have been looking for you for
just sixty-three mortal years.'

"'Excuse me,' I returned, as nonchalantly
as I could, considering the fact that I was
beginning to be annoyed—'excuse me, but
that statement seems to indicate that I was
born famous, which I'm inclined to doubt.
Inasmuch as I am not yet fifty years old, I
cannot understand how it has come to pass
that you have been looking for me for sixty-
three years.'

"'Nevertheless, my statement was correct,' said he. 'I have been looking for
you for sixty-three years, but not for you as
you.'

"This made me laugh, although it added
slightly to my nervousness, which was now
beginning to return. To have a man with a
tin box in his hand tell me he had been
looking for me for thirteen years longer
than I had lived, and then to have him add
that it was not, however, me as myself that
he wanted, was amusing in a sense, and yet
I could not help feeling that it would be a

relief to know that the tin box did hold a drinking-cup, and not dynamite.

"'You seem to speak English,' I said, in answer to this remark, 'and I have always thought I understood that language pretty well, but you'll excuse me if I say that I don't see your point.'

"'Why is it that great men are so frequently obtuse?' he said, languidly, giving the ground such a push with his toe that it set the hammock swinging furiously. 'When I say that I have searched for you all these years, but not for you as you, I mean not for you as Dr. Carey, not for you as an individual, but for you as the possessor of a very rare eye.'

"'Go on,' I said, feebly, and rubbed my forehead, thinking perhaps my brains had got into a tangle, and were responsible for this extraordinary affair. 'What is the peculiar quality which makes my eye so rare?'

"'There is only one pair of eyes like them in the world, that I know of,' said the stranger, 'and I have visited all lands in search of them and experimented with all kinds of eyes.'

"'And I am the proud possessor of that pair?' I queried, becoming slightly more interested.

"'Not you,' said he. 'You and I together possess that pair, however.'

"'You and I?' I cried.

"'Yes,' said he. 'Your left eye and my right have the honor of being the only two unique eyes in the world.'

"'That's queer too,' I observed, a mixture of sarcasm and flippancy in my tones, I fear. 'You mean twonique, don't you?'

"The old gentleman drew himself up with dignity, made a gesture of impatience, and remarked that if I intended to be flippant he would leave me. Of course I would not hear of this, now that my curiosity had been aroused, and so I apologized.

"'Don't mention it,' he said. 'But, my dear doctor, you cannot imagine my sensations when I found your eye yesterday.'

"'Oh! You found it yesterday, did you?' I put in.

"'Yes,' he said. 'On Forty-third Street.'

"'I was on Forty-third Street yesterday,'

I replied, 'but really I was not conscious of the loss of my eye.'

"'Nobody said you had lost it,' said my visitor. 'I only said I had found it. I mean by that that I found it as Columbus found America. America was not necessarily lost before it was found. I had the good fortune to be passing through the street as you left your club. I glanced into your face as I passed, caught sight of your eye, and my heart stood still. There at last was that for which I had so long and so earnestly searched, and so overcome was I with joy at my discovery that I seemed to lose all power of speech, of locomotion, or of sane thought, and not until you had passed entirely out of sight did I return really to my senses. Then I rushed madly into the club-house I had seen you leave a few moments before, described you to the man at the door, learned your name and address, and—well, here I am.'

"'And what does all this extraordinary nonsense lead up to?' I asked. 'What do you intend to do about my eye? Do you wish to borrow it, buy it, or steal it?'

"'Doctor Carey,' said my visitor, sadly, 'I shall not live very long. I have reason to believe that another summer will find me in my grave, and I do not want to die without imparting to the world the news of a marvellous discovery I have made—the details of a wonderful invention that I have not only conceived, but have actually put into working order. *I*, an unknown man— too old to be able to refute the charge of senility were any one disposed to question the value of my statements—could announce to the world my great discovery a thousand times a day, and very properly the world would decline to believe in me. The world would cry humbug, and I should have been unable, had I failed to find you, to convince the world that I was not a humbug. With the discovery of your eye, all that is changed. I shall have an ally in you, and that is valuable for the reason that your statements, whatever they may be, will always be entitled to and will receive respectful attention. Here in this box is my invention. I shall let you discover its marvellous power for yourself, hoping that when you have dis-

covered its power, you will tell the world of
it, and of its inventor.'

"With that," said the doctor, "the old
fellow handed me the tin box, which I
opened with considerable misgivings as to
possible results.   There was no explosion,
however.   The cover came off easily enough,
and on the inside was a curiously shaped
telescope, not a drinking-cup, as I had at
first surmised.

"'Why, it's a telescope, isn't it?' I said.

"'Yes.   What did you suppose it was?'
he asked.

"'I hadn't an idea,' I replied, not exactly
truthfully.   'But it can't be good for much
in this shape,' I added, for, as I pulled the
parts out and got it to its full length, I found
that each section was curved, and that the
whole formed an arc, which, though scarcely
perceptible, nevertheless should, it seemed
to me, have interfered with the utility of the
instrument.

"'That's the point I want you to establish
one way or the other,' said my visitor, getting up out of the hammock, and pacing
nervously up and down the lawn.   'To my

eye that telescope is a marvel, and is the result of years of experiment.   It fulfils my
expectations, and if your eye is what I think
it is, I shall at last have found another to
whom it will appear the treasure it appears
to me to be.   You have a tower on your
house, I see.   Let us go up on the roof of
the tower, and test the glass.   Then we
shall see if I claim too much for it.'

"The earnestness of the old gentleman
interested me hugely, and I led the way
through the garden to the house, up the
tower stairs to the roof, and then standing
there, looking across the river at the Palisades looming up like a huge fortress before me, I put the telescope to my eye.

"'I see absolutely nothing,' I said, after
vainly trying to fathom the depths of the
instrument.

"'Alas!' began the old gentleman; and
then he laughed, nervously.   'You are us-
ing the wrong eye.   Try the other one.   It
is your left eye that has the power to show
the virtues of this glass.'

"I obeyed his order, and then a most
singular thing happened.   Strange sights

met my gaze.   At first I could see nothing
but the Palisades opposite me, but in an
instant my horizon seemed to broaden, the
vista through the telescope deepened, and
before I knew it my sight was speeding,
now through a beautiful country, over fields,
hills, and valleys ; then on through great
cities, out to and over a broad, gently undulating stretch which I at once recognized as
the prairie lands of the west.   In a minute
more I began to catch the idea of this
wonderful glass, for I now saw rising up
before me the wonderful beauties of the
Yosemite, and then, like a flash of the
lightning, my vision passed over the Sierra
Nevada range, my eye swept down upon
San Francisco, and was soon speeding over
the waters of the Pacific.

"Two minutes later I saw the strange
pagodas of the Chinese rising before me.
Sweeping my glass to the north, bleak
Siberia met my gaze; then to the south I
saw India, her jungles, her waste places.
Not long after, a most awful sight met my
gaze.   I saw a huge ship at the moment of
foundering in the Indian Ocean.   Horrified,

I turned my glass again to the north, and
the minarets of Stamboul rose up before
me ; then the dome of St. Peter's at Rome ;
then Paris ; then London ; then the Altantic
Ocean.   I levelled my glass due west, and
finally I could see nothing but one small,
black speck—as like to a fleck of dust as to
anything else—on the lens at the other end.
With a movement of my hand, I tried to wipe
it off, but it still remained, and, in answer to
a chuckle at my side, I put the glass down.

"'It is the most extraordinary thing I
ever saw,' I said.

"'Yes, it is,' said the other.

"'One can almost see around the world
with it,' I cried, breathless nearly with enthusiasm.

"'One can — quite,' said the inventor,
calmly.

"'Nonsense !' I said.   'Don't claim too
much, my friend.'

"'It is true,' said he.   'Did you notice a
speck on the glass?   I am sure you did, for
you tried to remove it.'

"'Yes,' said I, 'I did.   But what of it?
What does that signify ?'

"'It proves what I said,' he answered. 'You did see all the way around the world with that glass. The black spot on the lens that you thought was a piece of dust was the back of your own head.'

"'Nonsense, my boy! The back of my head is bigger than that,' I said.

"'Certainly it is,' he responded; 'but you must make some allowance for perspective. The back of your head is a trifle less than twenty-four thousand miles from the end of your nose the way you were looking at it.'"

"You mean to say——" began the lieutenant, as the doctor paused to chalk his cue.

"Never mind what I mean to say," said the doctor. "Reflect upon what I have said."

"But the man and the telescope—what became of them?" asked the lieutenant.

"I was about to tell you that. The old fellow who had made this marvellous glass, which to two eyes that he knew of, and to only two, would work as was desired, feeling that he was about to die, had come to me to offer the glass for sale on two con-

siderations. One was a consideration of
$25. The other was that I would leave no
stone unturned to discover a possible third
person younger than myself with an eye
similar to those we had, to whom at my
death the glass should be transmitted, ex-
acting from him the promise that he too
would see that it was passed along in the
same manner into the hands of posterity.
I was also to acquaint the world with the
story of the glass and the name of its inventor to the fullest extent possible."

"And you, of course, accepted?"

"I did," said the doctor; "but having no
money in my pocket, I went down into the
house to borrow it of my wife, and upon my
return to the roof, found no trace of the
glass, the old man, or the roof either."

"What!" cried the lieutenant. "Are you
crazy?"

"No," smiled the doctor. "Not at all.
For the moment I reached the roof of the
house, I opened my eyes, and found myself
still swinging in the hammock under the
trees."

"And the moral?" queried the lieutenant.

"You promised a moral, or I should not have listened."

"Always have money in your pocket," replied the doctor, pocketing the last ball, and putting up his cue. "Then you are not apt to lose great bargains such as I lost for the want of $25."

"It's a good idea," returned the lieutenant. "And you live up to it, I suppose?"

"I do," returned the oculist, tapping his pocket significantly. "Always!"

"Then," said the lieutenant, earnestly, "I wish you'd lend me a tenner, for really, doctor, I have gone clean broke."

A MIDNIGHT VISITOR

I DO not assert that what I am about to relate is in all its particulars absolutely true. Not, understand me, that it is not true, but I do not feel that I care to make an assertion that is more than likely to be received by a sceptical age with sneers of incredulity. I will content myself with a simple narration of the events of that evening, the memory of which is so indelibly impressed upon my mind, and which, were I able to do so, I should forget without any sentiments of regret whatsoever.

The affair happened on the night before I fell ill of typhoid fever, and is about the sole remaining remembrance of that immediate period left to me. Briefly the story is as follows :

Notwithstanding the fact that I was overworked in the practice of my profession—it

was early in March, and I was preparing my
contributions for the coming Christmas is-
sues of the periodicals for which I write—
I had accepted the highly honorable position of Entertainment Committeeman at one
of the small clubs to which I belonged.   I
accepted the office, supposing that the duties
connected with it were easy of performance,
and with absolutely no notion that the faith
of my fellow-committeemen in my judgment
was so strong that they would ultimately
manifest a desire to leave the whole pro-
gramme for the club's diversion in my hands.
This, however, they did; and when the
month of March assumed command of the
calendar I found myself utterly fagged out
and at my wits' end to know what style of
entertainment to provide for the club meeting to be held on the evening of the 15th
of that month.   I had provided already an
unusually taking variety of evenings, of
which one in particular, called the " Martyrs' Night," in which living authors writhed
through selections from their own works,
while an inhuman audience, every man of
whom had suffered even as the victims then

" MARTYRS' NIGHT "

suffered, sat on tenscore of camp-stools puff-
ing the smoke of twenty-five score of free
cigars into their faces, and gloating over
their misery, was extremely successful, and
had gained for me among my professional
brethren the enviable title of " Machiavelli
Junior." This performance, in fact, was the
one now uppermost in the minds of the club
members, having been the most recent of
the series; and it had been prophesied by
many men whose judgment was unassail-
able that no man, not even I, could ever
conceive of anything that could surpass it.
Disposed at first to question the accuracy
of a prophecy to the effect that I was, like
most others of my kind, possessed of limitations, I came finally to believe that perhaps, after all, these male Cassandras with
whom I was thrown were right. Indeed, the
more I racked my brains to think of something better than the "Martyrs' Night,"
the more I became convinced that in that
achievement I had reached the zenith of
my powers. The thing for me to do now
was to hook myself securely on to the zenith
and stay there. But how to do it? That

was the question which drove sleep from my
eyes, and deprived me for a period of six
weeks of my reason, my hair departing immediately upon the restoration thereof—a
not uncommon after-symptom of typhoid.

It was a typical March night, this one
upon which the extraordinary incident about
to be related took place.   It was the kind
of night that novelists use when they are
handling a mystery that in the abstract
would amount to nothing, but which in the
concrete of a bit of wild, weird, and windy
nocturnalism sends the reader into hysterics.
It may be—I shall not attempt to deny it—
that had it happened upon another kind of
an evening—a soft, mild, balmy June evening, for instance—my own experience would
have seemed less worthy of preservation in
the amber of publicity, but of that the reader
must judge for himself.   The fact alone remains that upon the night when my uncanny visitor appeared, the weather department
was apparently engaged in getting rid of its
remnants.   There was a large percentage
of withering blast in the general make-up
of the evening ; there were rain and snow,

which alternated in pattering upon my window-pane and whitening the apology for a wold that stands three blocks from my flat on Madison Square; the wind whistled as it always does upon occasions of this sort, and from all corners of my apartment, after the usual fashion, there seemed to come sounds of a supernatural order, the effect of which was to send cold chills off on their regular trips up and down the spine of their victim—in this instance myself. I wish that at the time the hackneyed quality of these sensations had appealed to me. That it did not do so was shown by the highly nervous state in which I found myself as my clock struck eleven. If I could only have realized at that hour that these symptoms were the same old threadbare premonitions of the appearance of a supernatural being, I should have left the house and gone to the club, and so have avoided the visitation then imminent. Had I done this, I should doubtless also have escaped the typhoid, since the doctors attributed that misfortune to the shock of my experience, which, in my then wearied state, I was unable to sustain—

and what the escape of typhoid would have meant to me only those who have seen the bills of my physician and druggist for services rendered and prescriptions compounded are aware. That my mind unconsciously took thought of spirits was shown by the fact that when the first chill came upon me I arose and poured out for myself a stiff bumper of old Reserve Rye, which I immediately swallowed; but beyond this I did not go. I simply sat there before my fire and cudgelled my brains for an idea whereby my fellow-members at the Gutenberg Club might be amused. How long I sat there I do not know. It may have been ten minutes; it may have been an hour—I was barely conscious of the passing of time — but I do know that the clock in the Dutch Reformed Church steeple at Twenty-ninth Street and Fifth Avenue was clanging out the first stroke of the hour of midnight when my door-bell rang.

Theretofore—if I may be allowed the word—the tintinnabulation of my door-bell had been invariably pleasing unto me. I am fond of company, and company alone was

betokened by its ringing, since my creditors gratify their passion for interviews at
my office, if perchance they happen to find
me there. But on this occasion—I could
not at the moment tell why—its clanging
seemed the very essence of discord. It
jangled with my nervous system, and as it
ceased I was conscious of a feeling of irri-
tability which is utterly at variance with my
nature outside of business hours. In the
office, for the sake of discipline, I frequently adopt a querulous manner, finding it necessary in dealing with office-boys, but the
moment I leave shop behind me I become
a different individual entirely, and have
been called a moteless sunbeam by those
who have seen only that side of my character. This, by-the-way, must be regarded
as a confidential communication, since I
am at present engaged in preparing a vest-
pocket edition of the philosophical works
of Schopenhauer in words of one syllable,
and were it known that the publisher had
intrusted the magnificent pessimism of that
illustrious juggler of words and theories to
a "moteless sunbeam" it might seriously

interfere with the sale of the work; and I may say, too, that this request that my confidence be respected is entirely disinterested, inasmuch as I declined to do the work on the royalty plan, insisting upon the payment of a lump sum, considerably in advance.

But to return. I heard the bell ring with a sense of profound disgust. I did not wish to see anybody. My whiskey was low, my quinine pills few in number; my chills alone were present in a profusion bordering upon ostentation.

"I'll pretend not to hear it," I said to myself, resuming my work of gazing at the flickering light of my fire—which, by-the-way, was the only light in the room.

"Ting-a-ling-a-ling" went the bell, as if in answer to my resolve.

"Confound the luck!" I cried, jumping from my chair and going to the door with the intention of opening it, an intention however which was speedily abandoned, for as I approached it a sickly fear came over me—a sensation I had never before known seemed to take hold of my being, and in-

"DO YOU HEAR THAT BOLT SLIDE?"

stead of opening the door, I pushed the bolt to make it the more secure.

"There's a hint for you, whoever you are!" I cried. "Do you hear that bolt slide, you?" I added, tremulously, for from the other side there came no reply—only a more violent ringing of the bell.

"See here!" I called out, as loudly as I could, "who are you, anyhow What do you want?"

There was no answer, except from the bell, which began again.

"Bell-wire's too cheap to steal!" I called again. "If you want wire, go buy it; don't try to pull mine out. It isn't mine, anyhow. It belongs to the house."

Still there was no reply, only the clanging of the bell; and then my curiosity overcame my fear, and with a quick movement I threw open the door.

"Are you satisfied now?" I said, angrily. But I addressed an empty vestibule. There was absolutely no one there, and then I sat down on the mat and laughed. I never was so glad to see no one in my life. But my laugh was short-lived.

"What made that bell ring?" I suddenly asked myself, and then the feeling of fear came upon me again. I gathered my somewhat shattered self together, sprang to my feet, slammed the door with such force that the corridors echoed to the sound, slid the bolt once more, turned the key, moved a heavy chair in front of it, and then fled like a frightened hare to the sideboard in my dining-room. There I grasped the decanter holding my whiskey, seized a glass from the shelf, and started to pour out the usual dram, when the glass fell from my hand, and was shivered into a thousand pieces on the hardwood floor; for, as I poured, I glanced through the open door, and there in my sanctum the flicker of a random flame divulged the form of a being, the eyes of whom seemed fixed on mine, piercing me through and through. To say that I was petrified but dimly expresses the situation. I was granitized, and so I remained, until by a more luminous flicker from the burning wood I perceived that the being wore a flaring red necktie.

"He is human," I thought; and with the

THE VISITOR ARRIVES

thought the tension on my nervous system relaxed, and I was able to feel a sufficiently well-developed sense of indignation to demand an explanation. "This is a mighty cool proceeding on your part," I said, leaving the sideboard and walking into the sanctum.

"Yes," he replied, in a tone that made me jump, it was so extremely sepulchral—a tone that seemed as if it might have been acquired in a damp corner of some cave off the earth. "But it's a cool evening."

"I wonder that a man of your coolness doesn't hire himself out to some refrigerating company," I remarked, with a sneer which would have delighted the soul of Cassius himself.

"I have thought of it," returned the being, calmly. "But never went any further. Summer-hotel proprietors have always outbid the refrigerating people, and they in turn have been laid low by millionaires, who have hired me on occasion to freeze out people they didn't like, but who have persisted in calling. I must confess, though, my dear Hiram, that you are not much warmer yourself — this greeting is hardly what I expected."

"Well, if you want to make me warmer," I retorted, hotly, "just keep on calling me Hiram. How the deuce did you know of that blot on my escutcheon, anyhow?" I added, for Hiram was one of the crimes of my family that I had tried to conceal, my parents having fastened the name of Hiram Spencer Carrington upon me at baptism for no reason other than that my rich bachelor uncle, who subsequently failed and became a charge upon me, was so named.

"I was standing at the door of the church when you were baptized," returned the visitor, "and as you were an interesting baby, I have kept an eye on you ever since. Of course I knew that you discarded Hiram as soon as you got old enough to put away childish things, and since the failure of your uncle I have been aware that you desired to be known as Spencer Carrington, but to me you are, always have been, and always will be, Hiram."

"Well, don't give it away," I pleaded. "I hope to be famous some day, and if the

American newspaper paragrapher ever got
hold of the fact that once in my life I was
Hiram, I'd have to Hiram to let me alone."

"That's a bad joke, Hiram," said the visitor, "and for that reason I like it, though I
don't laugh.   There is no danger of your
becoming famous if you stick to humor of
that sort."

"Well, I'd like to know," I put in, my
anger returning—"I'd like to know who in
Brindisi you are, what in Cairo you want,
and what in the name of the seventeen
hinges of the gates of Singapore you are
doing here at this time of night?"

"When you were a baby, Hiram, you had
blue eyes," said my visitor.   " Bonny blue
eyes, as the poet says."

"What of it?" I asked.

"This," replied my visitor.   "If you have
them now, you can very easily see what I am
doing here. *I am sitting down and talking
to you.*"

"Oh, are you?" I said, with fine scorn.
"I had not observed that.   The fact is, my
eyes were so weakened by the brilliance of
that necktie of yours that I doubt I could

see anything—not even one of my own jokes. It's a scorcher, that tie of yours.   In fact, I never saw anything so red in my life."

"I do not see why you complain of my tie," said the visitor. "Your own is just as bad."

"Blue is never so withering as red," I retorted, at the same time caressing the scarf I wore.

"Perhaps not—but—ah—if you will look in the glass, Hiram, you will observe that your point is not well taken," said my vis-à-vis, calmly.

I acted upon the suggestion, and looked upon my reflection in the glass, lighting a match to facilitate the operation.   I was horrified to observe that my beautiful blue tie, of which I was so proud, had in some manner changed, and was now of the same aggressive hue as was that of my visitor, red even as a brick is red. To grasp it firmly in my hands and tear it from my neck was the work of a moment, and then in a spirit of rage I turned upon my companion.

"See here," I cried, "I've had quite enough of you. I can't make you out, and

"I LOOKED UPON MY REFLECTION IN THE GLASS"

I can't say that I want to. You know where the door is—you will oblige me by putting it to its proper use."

"Sit down, Hiram," said he, "and don't be foolish and ungrateful. You are behaving in a most extraordinary fashion, destroying your clothing and acting like a madman generally. What was the use of ripping up a handsome tie like that?"

"I despise loud hues. Red is a jockey's color," I answered.

"But you did not destroy the red tie," said he, with a smile. "You tore up your blue one—look. There it is on the floor. The red one you still have on."

Investigation showed the truth of my visitor's assertion. That flaunting streamer of anarchy still made my neck infamous, and before me on the floor, an almost unrecognizable mass of shreds, lay my cherished cerulean tie. The revelation stunned me; tears came into my eyes, and trickling down over my cheeks, fairly hissed with the feverish heat of my flesh. My muscles relaxed, and I fell limp into my chair.

"You need stimulant," said my visitor,

kindly. "Go take a drop of your Old Reserve, and then come back here to me. I've something to say to you."

"Will you join me?" I asked, faintly.

"No," returned the visitor. "I am so fond of whiskey that I never molest it. That act which is your stimulant is death to the rye. Never realized that, did you?"

"No, I never did," I said, meekly.

"And yet you claim to love it. Bah!" he said.

And then I obeyed his command, drained my glass to the dregs, and returned. "What is your mission?" I asked, when I had made myself as comfortable as was possible under the circumstances.

"To relieve you of your woes," he said.

"You are a homœopath, I observe," said I, with a sneer. "You are a homœopath in theory and an allopath in practice."

"I am not usually unintelligent," said he. "I fail to comprehend your meaning. Perhaps you express yourself badly."

"I wish you'd express yourself for Zululand," I retorted, hotly. "What I mean is, you believe in the *similia similibus* business,

THE RED TIE

but you prescribe large doses. I don't believe troubles like mine can be cured on
your plan. A man can't get rid of his stock
by adding to it."

"Ah, I see. You think I have added to
your troubles?"

"I don't think so," I answered, with a
fond glance at my ruined tie. "I know so."

"Well, wait until I have laid my plan before you, and see if you won't change your
mind," said my visitor, significantly.

"All right," I said. "Proceed. Only
hurry. I go to bed early, as a rule, and it's
getting quite early now."

"It's only one o'clock," said the visitor,
ignoring the sarcasm. "But I will hasten,
as I've several other calls to make before
breakfast."

"Are you a milkman?" I asked.

"You are flippant," he replied. "But,
Hiram," he added, "I have come here to
aid you in spite of your unworthiness. You
want to know what to provide for your club
night on the 15th. You want something
that will knock the 'Martyr's Night' silly."

"Not exactly that," I replied. "I don't

want anything so abominably good as to make all the other things I have done seem failures.   That is not good business."

"Would you like to be hailed as the discoverer of genius?   Would you like to be the responsible agent for the greatest exhibition of skill in a certain direction ever seen?   Would you like to become the most famous *impresario* the world has ever known?"

"Now," I said, forgetting my dignity under the enthusiasm with which I was inspired by my visitor's words, and infected more or less with his undoubtedly magnetic spirit—"now you're shouting."

"I thought so, Hiram.   I thought so, and that's why I am here.   I saw you on Wall Street to-day, and read your difficulty at once in your eyes, and I resolved to help you.   I am a magician, and one or two little things have happened of late to make me wish to prestidigitate in public.   I knew you were after a show of some kind, and I've come to offer you my services."

"Oh, pshaw!" I said.   "The members of the Gutenberg Club are men of brains—not

"NOT A CARD FELL"

children. Card tricks are hackneyed, and sleight-of-hand shows pall."

"Do they, indeed?" said the visitor. "Well, mine won't. If you don't believe it, I'll prove to you what I can do."

"I have no paraphernalia," I said.

"Well, I have," said he, and as he spoke, a pack of cards seemed to grow out of my hands. I must have turned pale at this unexpected happening, for my visitor smiled, and said:

"Don't be frightened. That's only one of my tricks. Now choose a card," he added, "and when you have done so, toss the pack in the air. Don't tell me what the card is; it alone will fall to the floor."

"Nonsense!" said I. "It's impossible."

"Do as I tell you."

I did as he told me, to a degree only. I tossed the cards in the air without choosing one, although I made a feint of doing so.

Not a card fell back to the floor. They every one disappeared from view in the ceiling. If it had not been for the heavy chair I had rolled in front of the door, I think I should have fled.

"How's that for a trick?" asked my visitor.

I said nothing, for the very good reason that my words stuck in my throat.

"Give me a little *crème de menthe*, will you, please?" said he, after a moment's pause.

"I haven't a drop in the house," I said, relieved to think that this wonderful being could come down to anything so earthly.

"Pshaw, Hiram!" he ejaculated, apparently in disgust. "Don't be mean, and, above all, don't lie. Why, man, you've got a bottle full of it in your hand! Do you want it all?"

He was right. Where it came from I do not know; but, beyond question, the graceful, slim-necked bottle was in my right hand, and my left held a liqueur-glass of exquisite form.

"Say," I gasped, as soon as I was able to collect my thoughts, "what are your terms?"

"Wait a moment," he answered. "Let me do a little mind-reading before we arrange preliminaries."

"I haven't much of a mind to read to-night," I answered, wildly.

"" GRAB HOLD OF ME, BOYS ""

"You're right there," said he. "It's like a dime novel, that mind of yours to-night. But I'll do the best I can with it. Suppose you think of your favorite poem, and after turning it over in your mind carefully for a few minutes, select two lines from it, concealing them, of course, from me, and I will tell you what they are."

Now my favorite poem, I regret to say, is Lewis Carroll's "Jabberwock," a fact I was ashamed to confess to an utter stranger, so I tried to deceive him by thinking of some other lines. The effort was hardly successful, for the only other lines I could call to mind at the moment were from Rudyard Kipling's rhyme, "The Post that Fitted," and which ran,

"Year by year, in pious patience, vengeful Mrs. Boffin sits
Waiting for the Sleary babies to develop Sleary's fits."

"Humph!" ejaculated my visitor. "You're a great Hiram, you are."

And then rising from his chair and walking to my "poet's corner," the magician selected two volumes.

"There," said he, handing me the *Departmental Ditties*. "You'll find the lines you tried to fool me with at the foot of page thirteen. Look."

I looked, and there lay that vile Sleary sentiment, in all the majesty of type, staring me in the eyes.

"And here," added my visitor, opening *Alice in the Looking-Glass* — "here is the poem that to your mind holds all the philosophy of life :

> "'Come to my arms, my beamish boy,
> He chortled in his joy.'"

I blushed and trembled. Blushed that he should discover the weakness of my taste, trembled at his power.

"I don't blame you for coloring," said the magician. "But I thought you said the Gutenberg was made up of men of brains? Do you think you could stay on the rolls a month if they were aware that your poetic ideals are summed up in the 'Jabberwock' and 'Sleary's Fits'?"

"My taste might be far worse," I answered.

"I MUST HAVE FAINTED"

"Yes, it might. You might have stooped to liking some of your own verses. I ought really to congratulate you, I suppose," retorted the visitor, with a sneering laugh.

This roused my ire again.

"Who are you, anyhow, that you come here and take me to task?" I demanded, angrily. "I'll like anything I please, and without asking your permission. If I cared more for the *Peterkin Papers* than I do for Shakespeare, I wouldn't be accountable to you, and that's all there is about it."

"Never mind who I am," said the visitor. "Suffice to say that I am myself. You'll know my name soon enough. In fact, you will pronounce it involuntarily the first thing when you wake in the morning, and then—" Here he shook his head ominously, and I felt myself grow rigid with fright in my chair. "Now for the final trick," he said, after a moment's pause. "Think of where you would most like to be at this moment, and I'll exert my power to put you there. Only close your eyes first."

I closed my eyes and wished. When I opened them I was in the billiard-room of the Gutenberg Club with Perkins and Tompson.

"For Heaven's sake, Spencer," they said, in surprise, "where did you drop in from? Why, man, you are as white as a sheet. And what a necktie! Take it off!"

"Grab hold of me, boys, and hold me fast," I pleaded, falling on my knees in terror. "If you don't, I believe I'll die."

The idea of returning to my sanctum was intolerably dreadful to me.

"Ha! ha!" laughed the magician, for even as I spoke to Perkins and Tompson I found myself seated opposite my infernal visitor in my room once more. "They couldn't keep you an instant with me summoning you back."

His laughter was terrible; his frown was pleasanter; and I felt myself gradually losing control of my senses.

"Go," I cried. "Leave me, or you will have the crime of murder on your conscience."

"I have no con—" he began; but I heard no more.

That is the last I remember of that fear-

THE MIND-READING FEATS ON THE CLUB'S BUTLER

ful night. I must have fainted, and then
have fallen into a deep slumber.

When I waked it was morning, and I was
alone, but undressed and in bed, uncon-
scionably weak, and surrounded by medi-
cine bottles of many kinds. The clock on
the mantle on the other side of the room
indicated that it was after ten o'clock.

"*Great Beelzebub!*" I cried, taking note
of the hour. "I've an engagement with
Barlow at nine."

And then a sweet-faced woman, who, I
afterwards learned, was a professional nurse,
entered the room, and within an hour I realized two facts. One was that I had lain ill
for many days, and that my engagement
with Barlow was now for six weeks unful-
filled ; the other, that my midnight visitor
was none other than—

And yet I don't know. His tricks certainly were worthy of that individual ; but
Perkins and Tompson assert that I never
entered the club that night, and surely if
my visitor was Beelzebub himself he would
not have omitted so important a factor of
success as my actual presence in the billiard-

room on that occasion would have been;
and, besides, he was altogether too cool to
have come from his reputed residence.

Altogether I think the episode most unaccountable, particularly when I reflect that
while no trace of my visitor was discover-
able in my room the next morning, as my
nurse tells me, my blue necktie was in reality found upon the floor, crushed and torn
into a shapeless bundle of frayed rags.

As for the club entertainment, I am told
that, despite my absence, it was a wonderful
success, redeemed from failure, the treasurer
of the club said, by the voluntary services
of a guest, who secured admittance on one
of my cards, and who executed some sleight-
of-hand tricks that made the members trem-
ble, and whose mind-reading feats performed
on the club's butler not only made it necessary for him to resign his office, but disclosed
to the House Committee the whereabouts
of several cases of rare wines that had mys-
teriously disappeared.

A QUICKSILVER CASSANDRA

It was altogether queer, and Jingleberry to this day does not entirely understand it. He had examined his heart as carefully as he knew how, and had arrived at the entirely reasonable conclusion that he was in love. He had every symptom of that malady. When Miss Marian Chapman was within range of his vision there was room for no one else there. He suffered from that peculiar optical condition which enabled him to see but one thing at a time when she was present, and she was that one thing, which was probably the reason why in his mind's eye she was the only woman in the world, for Marian was ever present before Jingleberry's mental optic. He had also examined as thoroughly as he could in hypothesis the heart of this "only woman," and he had — or thought he had, which amounts to the same thing—reason to believe that she reciprocated his affection. She certainly seemed glad always when he was about; she called him by his first name, and sometimes quarrelled with him as she quarrelled with no one else, and if that wasn't a sign of love in woman, then Jingleberry had studied the sex all his years— and they were thirty-two—for nothing. In short, Marian behaved so like a sister to him that Jingleberry, knowing how dreams and women go by contraries, was absolutely sure that a sister was just the reverse from that relationship which in her heart of hearts she was willing to assume towards him, and he was happy in consequence. Believing this, it was not at all strange that he should make up his mind to propose marriage to her, though, like many other men, he was somewhat chicken-hearted in coming to the point. Four times had he called upon Marian for the sole purpose of asking her to become his wife, and four times had he led up to the point and then talked about something else. What quality it is in man that makes a coward of him in the presence of one he considers his dearest friend is not within the province of this narrative to determine, but Jingleberry had it in its most virulent form. He had often got so far along in his proposal as " Marian—er—will you—will you—," and there he had as often stopped, contenting himself with such common-place conclusions as " go to the matinée with me to-morrow ?" or " ask your father for me if he thinks the stock market is likely to strengthen soon ?" and other amazing substitutes for the words he so ardently desired, yet feared, to utter.   But this afternoon— the one upon which the extraordinary events about to be narrated took place — Jingleberry had called resolved not to be balked in his determination to learn his fate.   He had come to propose, and propose he would, *ruat cœlum.* His confidence in a successful termination to his suit had been reinforced that very morning by the receipt of a note from Miss Chapman asking him to dine with her parents and herself that evening, and to accompany them after dinner to the opera. Surely that meant a great deal, and Jingleberry conceived that the time was ripe for a blushing "yes" to his long-

deferred question.   So he was here in the
Chapman parlor waiting for the young lady
to come down and become the recipient
of the "interesting interrogatory," as it is
called in some sections of Massachusetts.

"I'll ask her the first thing," said Jingleberry, buttoning up his Prince Albert, as
though to impart a possibly needed stiffen-
ing to his backbone.   "She will say yes,
and then I shall enjoy the dinner and the
opera so much the more.   Ahem! I wonder
if I am pale—I feel sort of—um— There's
a mirror.   That will tell."   Jingleberry
walked to the mirror—an oval, gilt-framed
mirror, such as was very much the vogue fifty
years ago, for which reason alone, no doubt,
it was now admitted to the gold-and-white
parlor of the house of Chapman.

"Blessed things these mirrors," said Jingleberry, gazing at the reflection of his face.
"So reassuring. I'm not at all pale. Quite
the contrary.   I'm red as a sunset.   Good
omen that!   The sun is setting on my
bachelor days—and my scarf is crooked.
Ah!"

The ejaculation was one of pleasure, for

pictured in the mirror Jingleberry saw the
form of Marian entering the room through
the portières.

" How do you do, Marian? been admir-
ing myself in the glass," he said, turning to
greet her. " I—er—"

Here he stopped, as well he might, for
he addressed no one. Miss Chapman was
nowhere to be seen.

" Dear me !" said Jingleberry, rubbing his
eyes in astonishment. " How extraordinary!
I surely thought I saw her—why, I did see
her—that is, I saw her reflection in the gla—
Ha ! ha ! She caught me gazing at myself
there and has hidden."

He walked to the door and drew the
portière aside and looked into the hall.
There was no one there. He searched every
corner of the hall and of the dining-room at
its end, and then returned to the parlor, but
it was still empty. And then occurred the
most strangely unaccountable event in his
life.

As he looked about the parlor, he for the
second time found himself before the mirror, but the reflection therein, though it was

of himself, was of himself with his back
turned to his real self, as he stood gazing
amazedly into the glass ; and besides this,
although Jingleberry was alone in the real
parlor, the reflection of the dainty room
showed that there he was not so, for seated
in her accustomed graceful attitude in the
reflected arm-chair was nothing less than
the counterfeit presentment of Marian Chapman herself.

It was a wonder Jingleberry's eyes did
not fall out of his head, he stared so. What
a situation it was, to be sure, to stand there
and see in the glass a scene which, as far
as he could observe, had no basis in reality;
and how interesting it was for Jingleberry
to watch himself going through the form of
chatting pleasantly there in the mirror's
depths with the woman he loved ! It almost
made him jealous, though, the reflected
Jingleberry was so entirely independent of
the real Jingleberry. The jealousy soon
gave way to consternation, for, to the won-
dering suitor, the independent reflection was
beginning to do that for which he himself
had come. In other words, there was a pro-

posal going on there in the glass, and Jingleberry enjoyed the novel sensation of seeing
how he himself would look when passing
through a similar ordeal.   Altogether, however, it was not as pleasing as most novel-
ties are, for there were distinct signs in the
face of the mirrored Marian that the mirrored Jingleberry's words were distasteful
to her, and that the proposition he was
making was not one she could entertain
under any circumstances.   She kept shaking her head, and the more she shook it,
the more the glazed Jingleberry seemed to
implore her to be his.   Finally, Jingleberry
saw his quicksilver counterpart fall upon
his knees before Marian of the glass, and
hold out his arms and hands towards her in
an attitude of prayerful despair, whereupon
the girl sprang to her feet, stamped her left
foot furiously upon the floor, and pointed
the unwelcome lover to the door.

Jingleberry was fairly staggered.   What
could be the meaning of so extraordinary a
freak of nature?   Surely it must be pro-
phetic.   Fate was kind enough to warn him
in advance, no doubt; otherwise it was a

trick. And why should she stoop to play so paltry a trick as that upon him? Surely fate would not be so petty. No. It was a warning. The mirror had been so affected by some supernatural agency that it divined and reflected that which was to be instead of confining itself to what Jingleberry called "simultaneity." It led instead of following or acting coincidently with the reality, and it was the part of wisdom, he thought, for him to yield to its suggestion and retreat; and as he thought this, he heard a soft sweet voice behind him.

"I hope you haven't got tired of waiting, Tom," it said; and, turning, Jingleberry saw the unquestionably real Marian standing in the doorway.

"No," he answered, shortly. "I—I have had a pleasant—very entertaining ten minutes; but I—I must hurry along, Marian," he added. "I only came to tell you that I have a frightful headache, and—er—I can't very well manage to come to dinner or go to the opera with you to-night."

"Why, Tom," pouted Marian, "I am awfully disappointed! I had counted on you, and now my whole evening will be spoiled. Don't you think you can rest a little while, and then come?"

"Well, I—I want to, Marian," said Jingleberry; "but, to tell the truth, I—I really am afraid I am going to be ill; I've had such a strange experience this afternoon. I—"

"Tell me what it was," suggested Marian, sympathetically; and Jingleberry did tell her what it was. He told her the whole story from beginning to end—what he had come for, how he had happened to look in the mirror, and what he saw there; and Marian listened attentively to every word he said. She laughed once or twice, and when he had done she reminded him that mirrors have a habit of reversing everything; and somehow or other Jingleberry's headache went, and—and—well, everything went!

THE GHOST CLUB

AN UNFORTUNATE EPISODE IN THE LIFE OF NO. 5010

NUMBER 5010 was at the time when I received the details of this story from his lips a stalwart man of thirty-eight, swart of hue, of pleasing address, and altogether the last person one would take for a convict serving a term for sneak-thieving. The only outer symptoms of his actual condition were the striped suit he wore, the style and cut of which are still in vogue at Sing Sing prison, and the closely cropped hair, which showed off the distinctly intellectual lines of his head to great advantage. He was engaged in making shoes when I first saw him, and so impressed was I with the contrast between his really refined features and grace of manner and those of his brutish-looking companions, that I asked my

"5010"

guide who he was, and what were the circumstances which had brought him to Sing
Sing.

"He pegs shoes like a gentleman," I said.

"Yes," returned the keeper. "He's
werry troublesome that way. He thinks
he's too good for his position. We can't
never do nothing with the boots he makes."

"Why do you keep him at work in the
shoe department?" I queried.

"We haven't got no work to be done in
his special line, so we have to put him at
whatever we can. He pegs shoes less badly than he does anything else."

"What was his special line?"

"He was a gentleman of leisure travellin'
for his health afore he got into the toils o'
the law. His real name is Marmaduke
Fitztappington De Wolfe, of Pelhamhurst-
by-the-Sea, Warwickshire. He landed in
this country of a Tuesday, took to collectin'
souvenir spoons of a Friday, was jugged
the same day, tried, convicted, and there
he sets. In for two years more."

"How interesting!" I said. "Was the
evidence against him conclusive?"

"Extremely.   A half-dozen spoons was found on his person."

"He pleaded guilty, I suppose?"

"Not him.   He claimed to be as inno-cent as a new-born babe.   Told a cock-and-bull story about havin' been deluded by spirits, but the judge and jury wasn't to be fooled.   They gave him every chance, too. He even cabled himself, the judge did, to Pelhamhurst-by-the-Sea, Warwickshire, at his own expense, to see if the man was an impostor, but he never got no reply.   There was them as said there wasn't no such place as Pelhamhurst-by-the-Sea in Warwickshire, but they never proved it."

"I should like very much to interview him," said I.

"It can't be done, sir," said my guide. "The rules is very strict."

"You couldn't—er—arrange an interview for me," I asked, jingling a bunch of keys in my pocket.

He must have recognized the sound, for he colored and gruffly replied, "I has me orders, and I obeys 'em."

"Just—er—add this to the pension fund,"

"PEGGING SHOES LIKE A GENTLEMAN"

I put in, handing him a five-dollar bill. "An interview is impossible, eh?"

"I didn't say impossible," he answered, with a grateful smile. "I said against the rules, but we has been known to make exceptions. I think I can fix you up."

Suffice it to say that he did "fix me up," and that two hours later 5010 and I sat down together in the cell of the former, a not too commodious stall, and had a pleasant chat, in the course of which he told me the story of his life, which, as I had surmised, was to me, at least, exceedingly interesting, and easily worth twice the amount of my contribution to the pension fund under the management of my guide of the morning.

"My real name," said the unfortunate convict, "as you may already have guessed, is not 5010. That is an alias forced upon me by the State authorities. My name is really Austin Merton Surrennes."

"Ahem!" I said. "Then my guide erred this morning when he told me that in reality you were Marmaduke Fitztappington De Wolfe, of Pelhamhurst-by-the-Sea, Warwickshire?"

Number 5010 laughed long and loud. "Of course he erred. You don't suppose that I would give the authorities my real name, do you? Why, man, I am a nephew! I have an aged uncle—a rich millionaire uncle—whose heart and will it would break were he to hear of my present plight. Both the heart and will are in my favor, hence my tender solicitude for him. I am inno-cent, of course—convicts always are, you know—but that wouldn't make any differ-ence. He'd die of mortification just the same. It's one of our family traits, that. So I gave a false name to the authorities, and secretly informed my uncle that I was about to set out for a walking trip across the great American desert, requesting him not to worry if he did not hear from me for a number of years, America being in a state of semi-civilization, to which mails outside of certain districts are entirely un-known. My uncle being an Englishman and a conservative gentleman, addicted more to reading than to travel, accepts the information as veracious and suspects noth-ing, and when I am liberated I shall return to him, and at his death shall become a conservative man of wealth myself. See?"

"But if you are innocent and he rich and influential, why did you not appeal to him to save you?" I asked.

"Because I was afraid that he, like the rest of the world, would decline to believe my defence," sighed 5010. "It was a good defence, if the judge had only known it, and I'm proud of it."

"But ineffectual," I put in. "And so, not good."

"Alas, yes! This is an incredulous age. People, particularly judges, are hard-headed practical men of affairs. My defence was suited more for an age of mystical tendencies. Why, will you believe it, sir, my own lawyer, the man to whom I paid eighteen dollars and seventy-five cents for championing my cause, told me the defence was rubbish, devoid even of literary merit. What chance could a man have if his lawyer even didn't believe in him?"

"None," I answered, sadly. "And you had no chance at all, though innocent?"

"Yes, I had one, and I chose not to take

it. I might have proved myself *non compos mentis ;* but that involved my making a fool of myself in public before a jury, and I have too much dignity for that, I can tell you. I told my lawyer that I should prefer a felon's cell to the richly furnished flat of a wealthy lunatic, to which he replied, 'Then all is lost!' And so it was. I read my defence in court. The judge laughed, the jury whispered, and I was convicted instanter of stealing spoons, when murder itself was no further from my thoughts than theft."

"But they tell me you were caught red-handed," said I. "Were not a half-dozen spoons found upon your person?"

"In my hand," returned the prisoner. "The spoons were in my hand when I was arrested, and they were seen there by the owner, by the police, and by the usual crowd of small boys that congregate at such embarrassing moments, springing up out of sidewalks, dropping down from the heavens, swarming in from everywhere. I had no idea there were so many small boys in the world until I was arrested, and found my-

5010 BECOMES EXCITED

self the cynosure of a million or more inno-
cent blue eyes."

"Were they all blue-eyed?" I queried,
thinking the point interesting from a scientific point of view, hoping to discover that
curiosity of a morbid character was always
found in connection with eyes of a specified
hue.

"Oh no ; I fancy not," returned my host.
"But to a man with a load of another fellow's spoons in his possession, and a pair
of handcuffs on his wrists, everything looks
blue."

"I don't doubt it," I replied.   "But—er
—just how, now, could you defend yourself
when every bit of evidence, and—you will
excuse me for saying so—conclusive evidence at that, pointed to your guilt?"

"The spoons were a gift," he answered.

"But the owner denied that."

"I know it ; that's where the beastly part
of it all came in.   They were not given to
me by the owner, but by a lot of mean, low-
down, practical-joke-loving ghosts."

Number 5010's anger as he spoke these
words was terrible to witness, and as he

strode up and down the floor of his cell and dashed his arms right and left, I wished for a moment that I was elsewhere. I should not have flown, however, even had the cell door been open and my way clear, for his suggestion of a supernatural agency in connection with his crime whetted my curiosity until it was more keen than ever, and I made up my mind to hear the story to the end, if I had to commit a crime and get myself sentenced to confinement in that prison for life to do so.

Fortunately, extreme measures of this nature were unnecessary, for after a few moments Surrennes calmed down, and seating himself beside me on the cot, drained his water-pitcher to the dregs, and began.

" Excuse me for not offering you a drink," he said, " but the wine they serve here while moist is hardly what a connoisseur would choose except for bathing purposes, and I compliment you by assuming that you do not wish to taste it."

" Thank you," I said. " I do not like to take water straight, exactly. I always dilute it, in fact, with a little of this."

Here I extracted a small flask from my pocket and handed it to him.

"Ah!" he said, smacking his lips as he took a long pull at its contents, "that puts spirit into a man."

"Yes, it does," I replied, ruefully, as I noted that he had left me very little but the flask; "but I don't think it was necessary for you to deprive me of all mine."

"No; that is, you can't appreciate the necessity unless you—er—you have suffered in your life as I am suffering. You were never sent up yourself?"

I gave him a glance which was all indignation. "I guess not," I said. "I have led a life that is above reproach."

"Good!" he replied. "And what a satisfaction that is, eh? I don't believe I'd be able to stand this jail life if it wasn't for my conscience, which is as clear and clean as it would be if I'd never used it."

"Would you mind telling me what your defence was?" I asked.

"Certainly not," said he, cheerfully. "I'd be very glad to give it to you. But you must remember one thing—it is copyrighted."

" Fire ahead !" I said, with a smile. " I'll respect your copyright. I'll give you a royalty on what I get for the story."

"Very good," he answered. " It was like this. To begin, I must tell you that when I was a boy preparing for college I had for a chum a brilliant fun-loving fellow named Hawley Hicks, concerning whose future various prophecies had been made. His mother often asserted that he would be a great poet ; his father thought he was born to be a great general ; our head - master at the Scarberry Institute for Young Gentlemen prophesied the gallows. They were all wrong; though, for myself, I think that if he had lived long enough almost any one of the prophecies might have come true. The trouble was that Hawley died at the age of twenty-three. Fifteen years elapsed. I was graduated with high honors at Brazenose, lived a life of elegant leisure, and at the age of thirty - seven broke down in health. That was about a year ago. My uncle, whose heir and constant companion I was, gave me a liberal allowance, and sent me off to travel. I came to America, landed in

"NO LESS A PERSON THAN HAWLEY HICKS"

New York early in September, and set about
winning back the color which had departed
from my cheeks by an assiduous devotion to
such pleasures as New York affords.   Two
days after my arrival, I set out for an airing
at Coney Island, leaving my hotel at four
in the afternoon.   On my way down Broadway I was suddenly startled at hearing my
name spoken from behind me, and appalled,
on turning, to see standing with outstretched
hands no less a person than my defunct
chum, Hawley Hicks."

"Impossible," said I.

"Exactly my remark," returned Number
5010.   "To which I added, 'Hawley Hicks,
it can't be you!'

"'But it is me,' he replied.

"And then I was convinced, for Hawley
never was good on his grammar.   I looked
at him a minute, and then I said, 'But, Hawley, I thought you were dead.'

"'I am,' he answered.   'But why should
a little thing like that stand between
friends?'

"'It shouldn't, Hawley,' I answered,
meekly; 'but it's condemnedly unusual, you

know, for a man to associate even with his best friends fifteen years after they've died and been buried.'

" ' Do you mean to say, Austin, that just because I was weak enough once to succumb to a bad cold, you, the dearest friend of my youth, the closest companion of my school-days, the partner of my childish joys, intend to go back on me here in a strange city ?'

" ' Hawley,' I answered, huskily, ' not a bit of it. My letter of credit, my room at the hotel, my dress suit, even my ticket to Coney Island, are at your disposal ; but I think the partner of your childish joys ought first to be let in on the ground-floor of this enterprise, and informed how the deuce you manage to turn up in New York fifteen years subsequent to your obsequies. Is New York the hereafter for boys of your kind, or is this some freak of my imagination ?' "

" That was an eminently proper question," I put in, just to show that while the story I was hearing terrified me, I was not altogether speechless.

"It was, indeed," said 5010; "and Hawley recognized it as such, for he replied at once.

"'Neither,' said he. 'Your imagination is all right, and New York is neither heaven nor the other place. The fact is, I'm spooking, and I can tell you, Austin, it's just about the finest kind of work there is. If you could manage to shuffle off your mortal coil and get in with a lot of ghosts, the way I have, you'd be playing in great luck.'

"'Thanks for the hint, Hawley,' I said, with a grateful smile; 'but, to tell you the truth, I do not find that life is entirely bad. I get my three meals a day, keep my pocket full of coin, and sleep eight hours every night on a couch that couldn't be more desirable if it were studded with jewels and had mineral springs.'

"'That's your mortal ignorance, Austin,' he retorted. 'I lived long enough to appreciate the necessity of being ignorant, but your style of existence is really not to be mentioned in the same cycle with mine. You talk about three meals a day, as if that were an ideal; you forget that with the eat-

ing your labor is just begun ; those meals
have to be digested, every one of 'em, and
if you could only understand it, it would
appall you to see what a fearful wear and
tear that act of digestion is.   In my life
you are feasting all the time, but with no
need for digestion.   You speak of money
in your pockets ; well, I have none, yet am
I the richer of the two.   I don't need money.   The world is mine.   If I chose to I
could pour the contents of that jeweller's
window into your lap in five seconds, but
cui bono ?   The gems delight my eye quite
as well where they are ; and as for travel,
Austin, of which you have always been fond,
the spectral method beats all.   Just watch
me !'

"I watched him as well as I could for a
minute," said 5010; "and then he disappeared.   In another minute he was before
me again.

"'Well,' I said, 'I suppose you've been
around the block in that time, eh ?'

"He roared with laughter.   'Around the
block ?' he ejaculated.   'I have done the
Continent of Europe, taken a run through

"'JUST WATCH ME'"

China, haunted the Emperor of Japan, and sailed around the Horn since I left you a minute ago.'

"He was a truthful boy in spite of his peculiarities, Hawley was," said Surrennes, quietly, "so I had to believe what he said. He abhorred lies."

"That was pretty fast travelling, though," said I. "He'd make a fine messenger-boy."

"That's so. I wish I'd suggested it to him," smiled my host. "But I can tell you, sir, I was astonished. 'Hawley,' I said, 'you always were a fast youth, but I never thought you would develop into this. I wonder you're not out of breath after such a journey.'

"'Another point, my dear Austin, in favor of my mode of existence. We spooks have no breath to begin with. Consequently, to get out of it is no deprivation. But, I say,' he added, 'whither are you bound?'

"'To Coney Island to see the sights,' I replied. 'Won't you join me?'

"'Not I,' he replied. 'Coney Island is tame. When I first joined the spectre band, it seemed to me that nothing could delight

me more than an eternal round of gay-
ety like that; but, Austin, I have changed.
I have developed a good deal since you and
I were parted at the grave.'

"'I should say you had,' I answered. 'I
doubt if many of your old friends would
know you.'

"'You seem to have had difficulty in so
doing yourself, Austin,' he replied, regret-
fully; 'but see here, old chap, give up
Coney Island, and spend the evening with
me at the club. You'll have a good time,
I can assure you.'

"'The club?' I said. 'You don't mean
to say you visions have a club?'

"'I do indeed; the Ghost Club is the
most flourishing association of choice spirits
in the world. We have rooms in every city
in creation; and the finest part of it is
there are no dues to be paid. The member-
ship list holds some of the finest names in
history—Shakespeare, Milton, Chaucer, Napoleon Bonaparte, Cæsar, George Washing-
ton, Mozart, Frederick the Great, Marc An-
tony—Cassius was black-balled on Cæsar's
account—Galileo, Confucius.'

NOAH AND DAVY CROCKETT

"'You admit the Chinese, eh?' I queried.

"'Not always,' he replied. 'But Con was such a good fellow they hadn't the heart to keep him out; but you see, Austin, what a lot of fine fellows there are in it.'

"'Yes, it's a magnificent list, and I should say they made a pretty interesting set of fellows to hear talk,' I put in.

"'Well, rather,' Hawley replied. 'I wish you could have heard a debate between Shakespeare and Cæsar on the resolution, "The Pen is mightier than the Sword;" it was immense.'

"'I should think it might have been,' I said. 'Which won?'

"'The sword party. They were the best fighters; though on the merits of the argument Shakespeare was 'way ahead.'

"'If I thought I'd stand a chance of seeing spooks like that, I think I'd give up Coney Island and go with you,' I said.

"'Well,' replied Hawley, 'that's just the kind of a chance you do stand. They'll all be there to-night, and as this is ladies' day, you might meet Lucretia Borgia, Cleopatra, and a few other feminine apparitions of considerable note.'

" 'That settles it. I am yours for the rest of the day,' I said, and so we adjourned to the rooms of the Ghost Club.

" These rooms were in a beautiful house on Fifth Avenue; the number of the house you will find on consulting the court records. I have forgotten it. It was a large, broad, brown-stone structure, and must have been over one hundred and fifty feet in depth. Such fittings I never saw before; everything was in the height of luxury, and I am quite certain that among beings to whom money is a measure of possibility no such magnificence is attainable. The paintings on the walls were by the most famous artists of our own and other days. The rugs on the superbly polished floors were worth fortunes, not only for their exquisite beauty, but also for their extreme rarity. In keeping with these were the furniture and bric-à-brac. In short, my dear sir, I had never dreamed of anything so dazzlingly, so superbly magnificent as that apartment into which I was ushered by

SOLOMON AND DOCTOR JOHNSON

the ghost of my quondam friend Hawley Hicks.

"At first I was speechless with wonder, which seemed to amuse Hicks very much."

" ' Pretty fine, eh?' he said, with a short laugh.

" ' Well,' I replied, in a moment, ' considering that you can get along without money, and that all the resources of the world are at your disposal, it is not more than half bad. Have you a library?'

"I was always fond of books," explained 5010 in parenthesis to me, "and so was quite anxious to see what the club of ghosts could show in the way of literary treasures. Imagine my surprise when Hawley informed me that the club had no collection of the sort to appeal to the bibliophile.

" ' No,' he answered, ' we have no library.'

" ' Rather strange,' I said, ' that a club to which men like Shakespeare, Milton, Edgar Allan Poe, and other deceased literati belong should be deficient in that respect.'

" ' Not at all,' said he. ' Why should we want books when we have the men them-

selves to tell their tales to us? Would you
give a rap to possess a set of Shakespeare if
William himself would sit down and rattle
off the whole business to you any time you
chose to ask him to do it? Would you follow Scott's printed narratives through their
devious and tedious periods if Sir Walter in
spirit would come to you on demand, and
tell you all the old stories over again in a
tenth part of the time it would take you to
read the introduction to one of them?'

"'I fancy not,' I said. 'Are you in such
luck?'

"'I am,' said Hawley; 'only personally I
never send for Scott or Shakespeare. I prefer something lighter than either—Douglas
Jerrold or Marryat. But best of all, I like
to sit down and hear Noah swap animal
stories with Davy Crockett. Noah's the
brightest man of his age in the club. Adam's
kind of slow.'

"'How about Solomon?' I asked, more
to be flippant than with any desire for information. I was much amused to hear
Hawley speak of these great spirits as if he
and they were chums of long standing.

MOZART TRIES HIS HAND AT THE BANJO

"'Solomon has resigned from the club,' he said, with a sad sigh. 'He was a good fellow, Solomon was, but he thought he knew it all until old Doctor Johnson got hold of him, and then he knuckled under. It's rather rough for a man to get firmly established in his belief that he is the wisest creature going, and then, after a couple of thousand years, have an Englishman come along and tell him things he never knew before, especially the way Sam Johnson delivers himself of his opinions. Johnson never cared whom he hurt, you know, and when he got after Solomon, he did it with all his might.'"

"I wonder if Boswell was there?" I ventured, interrupting 5010 in his extraordinary narrative for an instant.

"Yes, he was there," returned the prisoner. "I met him later in the evening; but he isn't the spook he might be. He never had much spirit anyhow, and when he died he had to leave his nose behind him, and that settled him."

"Of course," I answered. "Boswell with no nose to stick into other people's affairs

would have been like *Othello* with Desde-
mona left out. But go on. What did you
do next?"

"Well," 5010 resumed, "after I'd looked
about me, and drunk my fill of the magnificence on every hand, Hawley took me into
the music-room, and introduced me to Mozart and Wagner and a few other great com-
posers. In response to my request, Wagner
played an impromptu version of 'Daisy
Bell' on the organ. It was great; not
much like 'Daisy Bell,' of course; more
like a collision between a cyclone and a
simoom in a tin-plate mining camp, in fact,
but, nevertheless, marvellous. I tried to
remember it afterwards, and jotted down a
few notes, but I found the first bar took up
seven sheets of fool's-cap, and so gave it up.
Then Mozart tried his hand on a banjo for
my amusement, Mendelssohn sang a half-
dozen of his songs without words, and then
Gottschalk played one of Poe's weird stories
on the piano.

"Then Carlyle came in, and Hawley introduced me to him. He was a gruff old
gentleman, and seemingly anxious to have.

WAITING FOR THE CRITICS

Froude become an eligible, and I judged
from the rather fierce manner in which he
handled a club he had in his hand, that
there were one or two other men of promi-
nence still living he was anxious to meet.
Dickens, too, was desirous of a two-minute
interview with certain of his at present
purely mortal critics; and, between you and
me, if the wink that Bacon gave Shakespeare when I spoke of Ignatius Donnelly
meant anything, the famous cryptogram-
marian will do well to drink a bottle of the
elixir of life every morning before breakfast,
and stave off dissolution as long as he can.
There's no getting around the fact, sir,"
Surrennes added, with a significant shake
of the head, "that the present leaders of
literary thought with critical tendencies are
going to have the hardest kind of a time
when they cross the river and apply for ad-
mission to the Ghost Club. *I* don't ask for
any better fun than that of watching from a
safe distance the initiation ceremonies of
the next dozen who go over. And as an
Englishman, sir, who thoroughly believes in
and admires Lord Wolseley, if I were out of

jail and able to do it, I'd write him a letter, and warn him that he would better revise his estimates of certain famous soldiers no longer living if he desires to find rest in that mysterious other world whither he must eventually betake himself. They've got their swords sharpened for him, and he'll discover an instance when he gets over there in which the sword is mightier than the pen.

"After that, Hawley took me up-stairs and introduced me to the spirit of Napoleon Bonaparte, with whom I passed about twenty-five minutes talking over his victories and defeats. He told me he never could understand how a man like Wellington came to defeat him at Waterloo, and added that he had sounded the Iron Duke on the subject, and found him equally ignorant.

"So the afternoon and evening passed. I met quite a number of famous ladies— Catherine, Marie Louise, Josephine, Queen Elizabeth, and others. Talked architecture with Queen Anne, and was surprised to learn that she never saw a Queen Anne cottage. I took Peg Woffington down to supper, and altogether had a fine time of it."

NAPOLEON BONAPARTE AND THE DUKE OF
WELLINGTON

" But, my dear Surrennes," I put in at this point, " I fail to see what this has to do with your defence in your trial for stealing spoons."

" I am coming to that," said 5010, sadly. " I dwell on the moments passed at the club because they were the happiest of my life, and am loath to speak of what followed, but I suppose I must. It was all due to Queen Isabella that I got into trouble. Peg Woffington presented me to Queen Isabella in the supper-room, and while her majesty and I were talking, I spoke of how beautiful everything in the club was, and admired especially a half-dozen old Spanish spoons upon the side-board. When I had done this, the Queen called to Ferdinand, who was chatting with Columbus on the other side of the room, to come to her, which he did with alacrity. I was presented to the King, and then my troubles began.

" ' Mr. Surrennes admires our spoons, Ferdinand,' said the Queen.

" The King smiled, and turning to me observed, ' Sir, they are yours. Er—waiter, just do these spoons up and give them to Mr. Surrennes.'

"Of course," said 5010, " I protested against this; whereupon the King looked displeased.

"'It is a rule of our club, sir, as well as an old Spanish custom, for us to present to our guests anything that they may happen openly to admire. You are surely sufficiently well acquainted with the etiquette of club life to know that guests may not with propriety decline to be governed by the regulations of the club whose hospitality they are enjoying.'

"'I certainly am aware of that, my dear King,' I replied, 'and of course I accept the spoons with exceeding deep gratitude. My remonstrance was prompted solely by my desire to explain to you that I was unaware of any such regulation, and to assure you that when I ventured to inform your good wife that the spoons had excited my sincerest admiration, I was not hinting that it would please me greatly to be accounted their possessor.'

"'Your courtly speech, sir,' returned the King, with a low bow, 'is ample assurance of your sincerity, and I beg that you will

put the spoons in your pocket and say no
more. They are yours. *Verb. sap.*'

"I thanked the great Spaniard and said
no more, pocketing the spoons with no little
exultation, because, having always been a
lover of the quaint and beautiful, I was
glad to possess such treasures, though I
must confess to some misgivings as to the
possibility of their being unreal. Shortly
after this episode I looked at my watch and
discovered that it was getting well on towards eleven o'clock, and I sought out Hawley
for the purpose of thanking him for a delightful evening and of taking my leave. I
met him in the hall talking to Euripides on
the subject of the amateur stage in the
United States. What they said I did not
stop to hear, but offering my hand to Hawley informed him of my intention to depart.

"'Well, old chap,' he said, affectionately,
'I'm glad you came. It's always a pleasure
to see you, and I hope we may meet again
some time soon.' And then, catching sight
of my bundle, he asked, 'What have you
there?'

"I informed him of the episode in the

supper-room, and fancied I perceived a look of annoyance on his countenance.

"'I didn't want to take them, Hawley,' I said; 'but Ferdinand insisted.'

"'Oh, it's all right!' returned Hawley. 'Only I'm sorry! You'd better get along home with them as quickly as you can and say nothing; and, above all, don't try to sell them.'

"'But why?' I asked. 'I'd much prefer to leave them here if there is any question of the propriety of my—'

"Here," continued 5010, "Hawley seemed to grow impatient, for he stamped his foot angrily, and bade me go at once or there might be trouble. I proceeded to obey him, and left the house instanter, slamming the door somewhat angrily behind me. Hawley's unceremonious way of speeding his parting guest did not seem to me to be exactly what I had a right to expect at the time. I see now what his object was, and acquit him of any intention to be rude, though I must say if I ever catch him again, I'll wring an explanation from him for having introduced me into such bad company.

"As I walked down the steps," said 5010, "the chimes of the neighboring church were clanging out the hour of eleven. I stopped on the last step to look for a pos-- sible hansom-cab, when a portly gentleman accompanied by a lady started to mount the stoop. The man eyed me narrowly for a moment, and then, sending the lady up the steps, he turned to me and said,

" 'What are you doing here?'

" 'I've just left the club,' I answered. 'It's all right. I was Hawley Hicks's guest. Whose ghost are you?'

" 'What the deuce are you talking about?' he asked, rather gruffly, much to my sur- prise and discomfort.

" 'I tried to give you a civil answer to your question,' I returned, indignantly.

" 'I guess you're crazy—or a thief,' he rejoined.

" 'See here, friend,' I put in, rather im- pressively, 'just remember one thing. You are talking to a gentleman, and I don't take remarks of that sort from anybody, spook or otherwise. I don't care if you are the ghost of the Emperor Nero, if you give me any more of your impudence I'll dissipate you to the four quarters of the universe— see ?'

"Then he grabbed me and shouted for the police, and I was painfully surprised to find that instead of coping with a mysterious being from another world, I had two hun- dred and ten pounds of flesh and blood to handle.   The populace began to gather. The million and a half of small boys of whom I have already spoken — mostly street gamins, owing to the lateness of the hour — sprang up from all about us. Hansom-cab drivers, attracted by the noise of our altercation, drew up to the sidewalk to watch developments, and then, after the usual fifteen or twenty minutes, the blue- coat emissary of justice appeared.

"'Phat's dthis?' he asked.

"'I have detected this man leaving my house in a suspicious manner,' said my ad- versary.   'I have reason to suspect him of thieving.'

"'*Your* house!' I ejaculated, with fine scorn. 'I've got you there; this is the house of the New York Branch of the Ghost

Club. If you want it proved,' I added, turning to the policeman, 'ring the bell, and ask.'

" 'Oi t'ink dthat's a fair prophosition,' observed the policeman. 'Is the motion siconded ?'

" 'Oh, come now !' cried my captor. 'Stop this nonsense, or I'll report you to the department. This is my house, and has been for twenty years. I want this man searched.'

" 'Oi hov no warrant permithin' me to invistigate the contints ov dthe gintlemon's clothes,' returned the intelligent member of the force. 'But av yez 'll take yer solemn alibi dthat yez hov rayson t' belave the gintlemon has worked ony habeas corpush business on yure propherty, oi'll jug dthe blagyard.'

" 'I'll be responsible,' said the alleged owner of the house. 'Take him to the station.'

" 'I refuse to move,' I said.

" 'Oi'll not carry yez,' said the policeman, 'and oi'd advoise ye to furnish yure own locomotion. Av ye don't, oi'll use me club. Dthot's th' ounly waa yez 'll git dthe ambulanch.'

"'Oh, well, if you insist,' I replied, 'of course I'll go. I have nothing to fear.'

"You see," added 5010 to me, in parenthesis, "the thought suddenly flashed across my mind that if all was as my captor said, if the house was really his and not the Ghost Club's, and if the whole thing was only my fancy, the spoons themselves would turn out to be entirely fanciful; so I was all right—or at least I thought I was. So we trotted along to the police station. On the way I told the policeman the whole story. which impressed him so that he crossed himself a half-dozen times, and uttered numerous ejaculatory prayers—'Maa dthe shaints presharve us,' and 'Hivin hov mershy,' and others of a like import.

"'Waz dthe ghosht ov Dan O'Connell dthere?' he asked.

"Yes,' I replied. 'I shook hands with it.'

"'Let me shaak dthot hand,' he said, his voice trembling with emotion, and then he whispered in my ear: 'Oi belave yez to be innoshunt; but av yez ain't, for the love of Dan, oi'll let yez *esh*cape.'

"'LET ME SHAAK DTHOT HAND'"

"'Thanks, old fellow,' I replied. 'But I am innocent of wrong-doing, as I can prove.'

"Alas!" sighed the convict, "it was not to be so. When I arrived at the station-house, I was dumfounded to learn that the spoons were all too real. I told my story to the sergeant, and pointed to the monogram, 'G. C.,' on the spoons as evidence that my story was correct; but even that told against me, for the alleged owner's initials were G. C.—his name I withhold— and the monogram only served to substantiate his claim to the spoons. Worst of all, he claimed that he had been robbed on several occasions before this, and by midnight I found myself locked up in a dirty cell to await trial.

"I got a lawyer, and, as I said before, even he declined to believe my story, and suggested the insanity dodge. Of course I wouldn't agree to that. I tried to get him to subpœna Ferdinand and Isabella and Euripides and Hawley Hicks in my behalf, and all he'd do was to sit there and shake his head at me. Then I suggested going up to the Metropolitan Opera-house some fearful night as the clock struck twelve, and try to serve papers on Wagner's spook—all of which he treated as unworthy of a moment's consideration. Then I was tried, convicted, and sentenced to live in this beastly hole ; but I have one strong hope to buoy me up, and if that is realized, I'll be free to-morrow morning."

"What is that?" I asked.

"Why," he answered, with a sigh, as the bell rang summoning him to his supper— "why, the whole horrid business has been so weird and uncanny that I'm beginning to believe it's all a dream. If it is, why, I'll wake up, and find myself at home in bed ; that's all. I've clung to that hope for nearly a year now, but it's getting weaker every minute."

"Yes, 5010," I answered, rising and shaking him by the hand in parting; "that's a mighty forlorn hope, because I'm pretty wide awake myself at this moment, and can't be a part of your dream. The great pity is you didn't try the insanity dodge."

"Tut!" he answered. "That is the last resource of a weak mind."

A PSYCHICAL PRANK

I

WILLIS had met Miss Hollister but once,
and that, for a certain purpose, was suffi-
cient. He was smitten. She represented
in every way his ideal, although until he
had met her his ideal had been something
radically different. She was not at all
Junoesque, and the maiden of his dreams
had been decidedly so. She had auburn
hair, which hitherto Willis had detested.
Indeed, if the same hirsute wealth had
adorned some other woman's head, Willis
would have called it red. This shows how
completely he was smitten. She changed
his point of view entirely. She shattered
his old ideal and set herself up in its stead,
and she did most of it with a smile.

There was something, however, about
Miss Hollister's eyes that contributed to

the smiting of Willis's heart. They were great round lustrous orbs, and deep. So deep were they and so penetrating that Willis's affections were away beyond their own depth the moment Miss Hollister's eyes looked into his, and at the same time he had a dim and slightly uncomfortable notion that she could read every thought his mind held within its folds—or rather, that she could see how utterly devoid of thought that mind was upon this ecstatic occasion, for Willis's brain was set all agog by the sensations of the moment.

"By Jove!" he said to himself afterwards —for Willis, wise man that he could be on occasions, was his own confidant, to the exclusion of all others—"by Jove! I believe she can peer into my very soul; and if she can, my hopes are blasted, for she must be able to see that a soul like mine is no more worthy to become the affinity of one like hers than a mountain rill can hope to rival the Amazon."

Nevertheless, Willis did hope.

"Something may turn up, and perhaps— perhaps I can devise some scheme by means

of which my imperfections can be hidden
from her. Maybe I can put stained glass
over the windows of my soul, and keep her
from looking through them at my short-
comings. Smoked glasses, perhaps — and
why not? If smoked glasses can be used
by mortals gazing at the sun, why may they
not be used by me when gazing into those
scarcely less glorious orbs of hers?"

Alas for Willis! The fates were against
him. A far-off tribe of fates were in league
to blast his chances of success forever, and
this was how it happened :

Willis had occasion one afternoon to come
up town early. At the corner of Broadway
and Astor Place he entered a Madison Avenue car, paid his fare, and sat down in one
of the corner seats at the rear end of the
car. His mind was, as usual, intent upon
the glorious Miss Hollister. Surely no one
who had once met her could do otherwise
than think of her constantly, he reflected ;
and the reflection made him a bit jealous.
What business had others to think of her?
Impertinent, grovelling mortals! No man
was good enough to do that—no, not even

himself. But he could change. He could at least try to be worthy of thinking about her, and he knew of no other man who could. He'd like to catch any one else doing so little as mentioning her name!

"Impertinent, grovelling mortals!" he repeated.

And then the car stopped at Seventeenth Street, and who should step on board but Miss Hollister herself!

"The idea!" thought Willis. "By Jove! there she is—on a horse-car, too! How atrocious! One might as well expect to see Minerva driving in a grocer's wagon as Miss Hollister in a horse-car. Miserable, untactful world to compel Minerva to ride in a horse-cart, or rather Miss Hollister to ride in a grocer's car! Absurdest of absurdities!"

Here he raised his hat, for Miss Hollister had bowed sweetly to him as she passed on to the far end of the car, where she stood hanging on to a strap.

"I wonder why she doesn't sit down?" thought Willis; for as he looked about the car he observed that with the exception of the one he occupied all the seats were vacant. In fact, the only persons on board were Miss Hollister, the driver, the conductor, and himself.

" I think I'll go speak to her," he thought. And then he thought again : " No, I'd better not. She saw me when she entered, and if she had wished to speak to me she would have sat down here beside me, or opposite me perhaps. I shall show myself worthy of her by not thrusting my presence upon her. But I wonder why she stands ? She looks tired enough."

Here Miss Hollister indulged in a very singular performance. She bowed her head slightly at some one, apparently on the sidewalk, Willis thought, murmured something, the purport of which Willis could not catch, and sat down in the middle of the seat on the other side of the car, looking very much annoyed—in fact, almost unamiable.

Willis was more mystified than ever ; but his mystification was as nothing compared to his anxiety when, on reaching Forty-second Street, Miss Hollister rose, and sweeping by him without a sign of recognition, left the car.

"Cut, by thunder!" ejaculated Willis, in consternation. "And why, I wonder? Most incomprehensible affair. Can she be a woman of whims — with eyes like those? Never. Impossible. And yet what else can be the matter?"

Try as he might, Willis could not solve the problem. It was utterly past solution as far as he was concerned.

"I'll find out, and I'll find out like a brave man," he said, after racking his brains for an hour or two in a vain endeavor to get at the cause of Miss Hollister's cut. "I'll call upon her to-night and ask her."

He was true to his first purpose, but not to his second. He called, but he did not ask her, for Miss Hollister did not give him the chance to do so. Upon receiving his card she sent down word that she was out. Two days later, meeting him face to face upon the street, she gazed coldly at him, and cut him once more. Six months later her engagement to a Boston man was announced, and in the autumn following Miss Hollister of New York became Mrs. Barrows of Boston. There were cards, but Willis did not receive one of them. The cut was indeed complete and final. But why? That had now become one of the great problems of Willis's life. What had he done to be so badly treated?

II

A year passed by, and Willis recovered from the dreadful blow to his hopes, but he often puzzled over Miss Hollister's singular behavior towards him. He had placed the matter before several of his friends, and, with the exception of one of them, none was more capable of solving his problem than he. This one had heard from his wife, a school friend and intimate acquaintance of Miss Hollister, now Mrs. Barrows, that Willis's ideal had once expressed herself to the effect that she had admired Willis very much until she had discovered that he was not always as courteous as he should be.

"Courteous? Not as courteous as I should be?" retorted Willis. "When have I ever been anything else? Why, my dear Bronson," he added, "you know what my attitude towards womankind—as well as mankind—has always been. If there is a creature in the world whose politeness is his weakness, I am that creature. I'm the most courteous man living. When I play poker in my own rooms I lose money, because I've made it a rule never to beat my guests in cards or anything else."

"That isn't politeness," said Bronson. "That's idiocy."

"It proves my point," retorted Willis. "I'm polite to the verge of insanity. Not as courteous as I should be! Great Scott! What did I ever do or say to give her that idea?"

"I don't know," Bronson replied. "Better ask her. Maybe you overdid your politeness. Overdone courtesy is often worse than boorishness. You may have been so polite on some occasion that you made Miss Hollister think you considered her an inferior person. You know what the poet insinuated. Sorosis holds no fury like a woman condescended to by a man."

"I've half a mind to write to Mrs. Barrows and ask her what I did," said Willis.

"That would be lovely," said Bronson. "Barrows would be pleased."

"True. I never thought of that," replied Willis.

"You are not a thoughtful thinker," said Bronson, dryly. "If I were you I'd bide my time, and some day you may get an explanation. Stranger things have happened; and my wife tells me that the Barrowses are to spend the coming winter in New York. You'll meet them out somewhere, no doubt."

"No; I shall decline to go where they are. No woman shall cut me a second time — not even Mrs. Barrows," said Willis, firmly.

"Good! Stand by your colors," said Bronson, with an amused smile.

A week or two later Willis received an invitation from Mr. and Mrs. Bronson to dine with them informally. "I have some very clever friends I want you to meet," she wrote. "So be sure to come."

Willis went. The clever friends were Mr. and Mrs. Barrows; and, to the surprise of Willis, he was received most effusively by the quondam Miss Hollister.

"Why, Mr. Willis," she said, extending her hand to him. "How delightful to see you again!"

"Thank you," said Willis, in some confusion. "I — er — I am sure it is a very pleasant surprise for me. I — er — had no idea—"

"Nor I," returned Mrs. Barrows. "And really I should have been a little embarrassed, I think, had I known you were to be here. I—ha! ha!—it's so very absurd that I almost hesitate to speak of it—but I feel I must. I've treated you very badly."

"Indeed!" said Willis, with a smile. "How, pray?"

"Well, it wasn't my fault really," returned Mrs. Barrows; "but do you remember, a little over a year ago, my riding up-town on a horse-car—a Madison Avenue car—with you?"

"H'm!" said Willis, with an affectation of reflection. "Let me see; ah—yes—I think I do. We were the only ones on board, I believe, and—ah—"

Here Mrs. Barrows laughed outright. "You thought we were the only ones on

board, but—we weren't. The car was crowded," she said.

"Then I don't remember it," said Willis.
"The only time I ever rode on a horse-car
with you to my knowledge was—"

"I know; this was the occasion," inter-
rupted Mrs. Barrows. "You sat in a corner at the rear end of the car when I entered,
and I was very much put out with you because it remained for a stranger, whom I
had often seen and to whom I had, for rea-
sons unknown even to myself, taken a deep
aversion, to offer me his seat, and, what is
more, compel me to take it."

"I don't understand," said Willis. "We
were alone on the car."

"To your eyes we were, although at the
time I did not know it. To my eyes when
I boarded it the car was occupied by enough
people to fill all the seats. You returned
my bow as I entered, but did not offer me
your seat. The stranger did, and while I
tried to decline it, I was unable to do so.
He was a man of about my own age, and
he had a most remarkable pair of eyes.
There was no resisting them. His offer

was a command; and as I rode along and thought of your sitting motionless at the end of the car, compelling me to stand, and being indirectly responsible for my acceptance of courtesies from a total and disagreeable stranger, I became so very indignant with you that I passed you without recognition as soon as I could summon up courage to leave. I could not understand why you, who had seemed to me to be the soul of politeness, should upon this occasion have failed to do not what I should exact from any man, but what I had reason to expect of you."

"But, Mrs. Barrows," remonstrated Willis, "why should I give up a seat to a lady when there were twenty other seats unoccupied on the same car?"

"There is no reason in the world why you should," replied Mrs. Barrows. "But it was not until last winter that I discovered the trick that had been put upon us."

"Ah?" said Willis. "Trick?"

"Yes," said Mrs. Barrows. "It was a trick. The car was empty to your eyes, but crowded to mine with the astral bodies

of the members of the Boston Theosoph-
ical Society."

"Wha-a-at?" roared Willis.

"It is just as I have said," replied Mrs.
Barrows, with a silvery laugh. "They are
all great friends of my husband's, and one
night last winter he dined them at our
house, and who do you suppose walked in
first?"

"Madame Blavatsky's ghost?" suggested
Willis, with a grin.

"Not quite," returned Mrs. Barrows.
"But the horrible stranger of the horse-
car; and, do you know, he recalled the
whole thing to my mind, assuring me that
he and the others had projected their astral
bodies over to New York for a week, and
had a magnificent time unperceived by all
save myself, who was unconsciously psychic,
and so able to perceive them in their invisi-
ble forms."

"It was a mean trick on me, Mrs. Barrows," said Willis, ruefully, as soon as he
had recovered sufficiently from his surprise
to speak.

"Oh no," she replied, with a repetition

of her charming laugh, which rearoused in
Willis's breast all the regrets of a lost cause.
"They didn't intend it especially for you,
anyhow."

"Well," said Willis, "I think they did.
They were friends of your husband's, and
they wanted to ruin me."

"Ruin you?   And why should the friends
of Mr. Barrows have wished to do that?"
asked Mrs. Barrows, in astonishment.

"Because," began Willis, slowly and soft-
ly—"because they probably knew that from
the moment I met you, I—   But that is a
story with a disagreeable climax, Mrs. Barrows, so I shall not tell it.   How do you
like Boston?"

THE LITERARY REMAINS OF
THOMAS BRAGDON

I WAS much pained one morning last winter on picking up a copy of the *Times* to note therein the announcement of the death of my friend Tom Bragdon, from a sudden attack of la grippe. The news stunned me. It was like a clap of thunder out of a clear sky, for I had not even heard that Tom was ill; indeed, we had parted not more than four days previously after a luncheon together, at which it was I who was the object of his sympathy because a severe cold prevented my enjoyment of the whitebait, the fillet, the cigar, and indeed of everything, not even excepting Bragdon's conversation, which upon that occasion should have seemed more than usually enlivening, since he was in one of his most exuberant moods. His last words to me were, " Take care of yourself, Phil! I should hate to have you die, for force of habit is so strong with me that I shall forever continue to lunch with none but you, ordering two portions of everything, which I am sure I could not eat, and how wasteful that would be!" And now he had passed over the threshold into the valley, and I was left to mourn.

I had known Bragdon as a successful commission merchant for some ten or fifteen years, during which period of time we had been more or less intimate, particularly so in the last five years of his life, when we were drawn more closely together; I, attracted by the absolute genuineness of his character, his delightful fancy, and to my mind wonderful originality, for I never knew another like him; he, possibly by the fact that I was one of the very few who could entirely understand him, could sympathize with his peculiarities, which were many, and was always ready to enter into any one of his odd moods, and with quite as much spirit as he himself should display. It was an ideal friendship.

It had been our custom every summer to

"HE WAS IN AN UNUSUALLY EXUBERANT MOOD"

take what Bragdon called spirit trips together — that is to say, generally in the
early spring, Bragdon and I would choose
some out-of-the-way corner of the world for
exploration ; we would each read all the literature that we could find concerning the
chosen locality, saturate our minds with the
spirit, atmosphere, and history of the place,
and then in August, boarding a small
schooner-rigged boat belonging to Bragdon,
we would cruise about the Long Island
Sound or sail up and down the Hudson
River for a week, where, tabooing all other
subjects, we would tell each other all that
we had been able to discover concerning the
place we had decided upon for our imaginary visit. In this way we became tolerably
familiar with several places of interest which
neither of us had ever visited, and which, in
my case, financial limitations, and in Bragdon's, lack of time, were likely always to
prevent our seeing. As I remember the
matter, this plan was Bragdon's own, and
its first suggestion by him was received by
me with a smile of derision ; but the quaint-
ness of the idea in time won me over, and

after the first trial, when we made a spirit
trip to Beloochistan, I was so fascinated by
my experience that I eagerly looked forward
to a second in the series, and was always
thereafter only too glad to bear my share of
the trouble and expense of our annual jour-
neyings.   In this manner we had practically
circumnavigated this world and one or two
of the planets ; for, content as we were to
visit unseen countries in spirit only, we were
never hampered by the ordinary limitations
of travel, and where books failed to supply
us with information the imagination was
called into play. The universe was open
to us at the expense of a captain for our
sharpie, canned provisions for a week, and a
moderate consumption of gray matter in the
conjuring up of scenes with which neither
ourselves nor others were familiar. The
trips were refreshing always, and in the case
of our spirit journey through Italy, which at
that time neither of us had visited, but which
I have since had the good-fortune to see in
the fulness of her beauty, I found it to be
far more delightful than the reality.

"We'll go in," said Bragdon, when he

proposed the Italian tour, "by the St. Goth-
ard route, the description of which I will
prepare in detail myself. You can take the
lakes, rounding up with Como. I will follow with the trip from Como to Milan, and
Milan shall be my care. You can do Ve-
rona and Padua; I Venice. Then we can
both try our hands at Rome and Naples;
in the latter place, to save time, I will take
Pompeii, you Capri. Thence we can hark
back to Rome, thence to Pisa, Genoa, and
Turin, giving a day to Siena and some of the
quaint Etruscan towns, passing out by the
Mont Cenis route from Turin to Geneva.
If you choose you can take a run along the
Riviera and visit Monte Carlo. For my
own part, though, I'd prefer not to do that,
because it brings a sensational element into
the trip which I don't particularly care for.
You'd have to gamble, and if your imagination is to have full play you ought to lose
all your money, contemplate suicide, and all
that. I don't think the results would be
worth the mental strain you'd have to go
through, and I certainly should not enjoy
hearing about it. The rest of the trip,

though, we can do easily in five days, which
will leave us two for fishing, if we feel so
disposed. They say the blue-fish are bit-
ing like the devil this year."

I regret now that we did not include a
stenographer among the necessaries of our
spirit trips, for, as I look back upon that
Italian tour, it was well worthy of preservation in book form, particularly Bragdon's
contributions, which were so delightfully
imaginative that I cannot but rejoice that
he did not live to visit the scenes of which
he so eloquently spoke to me upon that
occasion. The reality, I fear, would have
been a sore disappointment to him, particularly in relation to Venice, concerning
which his notions were vaguely suggestive
of an earthly floating paradise.

"Ah, Philip," he said, as we cast anchor
one night in a little inlet near Milford, Con-
necticut, "I shall never forget Venice.
This," he added, waving his hand over the
silvery surface of the moonlit water—"this
reminds me of it. All is so still, so romantic, so beautiful. I arrived late at night,
and my first sensations were those of a man

"MORE BEAUTIFUL THAN THE REALITY"

who has entered a city of the dead. The
bustle, the noise and clatter, of a great city
were absent; nothing was there but the
massive buildings rising up out of the still,
peaceful waters like gigantic tombs, and as
my gondolier guided the sombre black craft
to which I had confided my safety and that
of my valise, gliding in and out along those
dark unlit streams, a great wave of melancholy swept over me, and then, passing from
the minor streets into the Grand Canal, the
melancholy was dispelled by the brilliant
scene that met my eyes — great floods of
light coming from everywhere, the brilliance
of each ray re-enforced by its reflection in
the silent river over which I was speeding.
It was like a glimpse of paradise, and when
I reached my palace I was loath to leave
the gondola, for I really felt as though I
could glide along in that way through all
eternity."

"You lived in a palace in Venice?" I
asked, somewhat amused at the magnificence of this imaginary tour.

"Certainly. Why not?" he replied. "I
could not bring myself to staying in a hotel,

Phil, in Venice. Venice is of a past age, when hotels were not, and to be thoroughly *en rapport* with my surroundings, I took up my abode in a palace, as I have said. It was on one of the side streets, to be sure, but it was yet a palace, and a beautiful one. And that street! It was a rivulet of beauty, in which could be seen myriads of golden-hued fish at play, which as the gondola passed to and fro would flirt into hiding until the intruder had passed out of sight in the Grand Canal, after which they would come slowly back again to render the silver waters almost golden with their brilliance."

"Weren't you rather extravagant, Tom?" I asked. " Palaces are costly, are they not?"

"Oh no," he replied, with as much gravity as though he had really taken the trip and was imparting information to a seeker after knowledge. " It was not extravagant when you consider that anything in Venice in the way of a habitable house is called a palace, and that there are no servants to be tipped; that your lights, candles all, cost you first price only, and not the profit of the landlord, plus that of the concierge, plus

that of the maid, plus several other small
but aggravatingly augmentative sums which
make your hotel bills seem like highway
robbery. No, living in a palace, on the
whole, is cheaper than living in a hotel; in-
cidentals are less numerous and not so costly; and then you are so independent. Mine
was a particularly handsome structure. I
believe I have a picture of it here."

Here Bragdon fumbled in his satchel for
a moment, and then dragged forth a small
unmounted photograph of a Venetian street
scene, and, pointing out an ornate structure
at the left of the picture, assured me that
that was his palace, though he had forgotten the name of it.

"By-the-way," he said, "let me say par-
enthetically that I think our foreign trips
will have a far greater *vraisemblance* if we
heighten the illusion with a few photographs,
don't you? They cost about a quarter
apiece at Blank's, in Twenty-third Street."

"A good idea that," I answered, amused at
the thoroughness with which Bragdon was
"doing" Venice. "We can remember what
we haven't seen so very much more easily."

"Yes," Bragdon said, "and besides, they'll keep us from exaggeration."

And then he went on to tell me of his month in Venice; how he chartered a gondola for the whole of his stay there from a handsome romantic Venetian youth, whose name was on a card Tom had had printed for the occasion, reading:

GIUSEPPE ZOCCO

GONDOLAS AT ALL HOURS

Cor. Grand Canal and Garibaldi St.

"Giuseppe was a character," Bragdon said. "One of the remnants of a by-gone age. He could sing like a bird, and at night he used to bring his friends around to the front of my palace and hitch up to one of the piles that were driven beside my doorstep, and there they'd sing their soft Italian melodies for me by the hour. It was better than Italian opera, and only cost me ten dollars for the whole season."

"And did this Giuseppe speak English,

GIUSEPPE ZOCCO

Tom?" I queried, "or did you speak Italian? I am curious to know how you got on together in a conversational sense."

"That is a point, my dear Phil," Bragdon replied, "that I have never decided. I have looked at it from every point of view, and it has baffled me. I have asked myself the question, which would be the more likely, that Giuseppe should speak English, or that I should speak Italian? It has seemed to me that the latter would be the better way, for, all things considered, an American produce-broker is more likely to be familiar with the Italian tongue than a Venetian gondola-driver with the English. On the other hand, we want our accounts of these trips to seem truthful, and you *know* that I am not familiar with Italian, and we do not either of us know that a possible Zocco would not be a fluent speaker of English. To be honest with you, I will say that I had hoped you would not ask the question."

"Well," I answered, "I'll withdraw it. As this is only a spirit trip we can each decide the point as it seems best to us."

" I think that is the proper plan," he said, and then, proceeding with his story, he described to me the marvellous paintings that adorned the walls of his palace; how he had tried to propel a gondola himself, and got a fall into the "deliciously tepid waters of the canal," as he called them, for his pains; and it seemed very real, so minute were the details into which he entered.

But the height of Bragdon's realism in telling his story of Venice was reached when, diving down into the innermost recesses of his vest pocket, he brought forth a silver filigree effigy of a gondola, which he handed me with the statement that it was for me.

"I got that in the plaza of St. Marc's. I had visited the cathedral, inspected the mosaic flooring, taken a run to the top of the campanile, fed the pigeons, and was just about returning to the palace, when I thought of you, Phil, getting ready to do Rome with me, and I thought to myself 'what a dear fellow he is!' and, as I thought that, it occurred to me that I'd like you to know I had you in mind at the time, and so I stopped in one of those brilliant little

shops on the plaza, where they keep everything they have in the windows, and bought
that. It isn't much, old fellow, but it's for
remembrance' sake."

I took it from him and pressed his hand
affectionately, and for a moment, as the little sharpie rose and fell with the rising and
falling of the slight undulating waves made
by the passing up to anchorage of a small
steam-tug, I almost believed that Tom had
been to Venice. I still treasure the little
filigree gondola, nor did I, when some years
later I visited Venice, see there anything for
which I would have exchanged that sweet
token of remembrance.

Bragdon, as will already have been surmised by you who read, was more of a hu-
morist than anything else, but the enthusiasm of his humor, its absolute spontaneity
and kindliness, gave it at times a semblance
to what might pass for true poetry. He was
by disposition a thoroughly sweet spirit,
and when I realized that he had gone before, and that the trips he and I had looked
forward to with such almost boyish delight
year by year were never more to be had,

my eyes grew wet, and for a time I was dis-
consolate; and yet one week later I was
laughing heartily at Bragdon.

He had appointed me, it was found when
his will was read, his literary executor.   I
fairly roared with mirth to think of Bragdon's having a literary executor, for, imaginative and humorous as he undoubtedly
was, he had been so thoroughly identified
in my mind with the produce business that
I could scarcely bring myself to think of
him in the light of a literary person.   Indeed, he had always seemed to me to have
an intolerance of literature.   I had taken
but half of a spirit trip with him when I discovered that he relied more upon his own
imagination for facts of interest than upon
what could be derived from books.   He
showed this trait no more strongly than
when we came, upon this same Italian tour
of which I have already written at some
length, to do Rome together, for I then discovered how imaginary indeed the trips
were from his point of view.   What seemed
to him as proper to be was, and neither history nor considerations of locality ever inter-

fered with the things being as he desired
them to be.   Had it been otherwise he never
would have endeavored to make me believe
that he had stood upon the very spot in the
Colosseum where Cæsar addressed the Ro-
man mob in impassioned words, exhorting
them to resist the encroachment upon their
liberties of the Pope !

At first it seemed to me that my late friend
was indulging in a posthumous joke, and I
paid his memory the compliment of seeing
the point.   But when, some days later, I
received a note from his executors stating
that they had found in the store-room of
Bragdon's house a large packing-box full of
papers and books, upon the cover of which
was tacked a card bearing my address, I
began to wonder whether or not, after all,
the imagination of my dead friend had really led him to believe that he possessed literary ability.

I immediately sent word to the executors
to have the box forwarded to me by express,
and awaited its coming with no little interest, and, it must be confessed, with some
anxiety; for I am apt to be depressed by

the literary lucubrations of those of my friends who, devoid of the literary quality, do yet persist in writing, and for as long a time as I had known Bragdon I had never experienced through him any sensations save those of exhilaration, and I greatly feared a posthumous breaking of the spell. Poet in feeling as I thought him, I could hardly imagine a poem written by my friend, and while I had little doubt that I could live through the reading of a novel or short prose sketch from his pen, I was apprehensive as to the effect of a possible bit of verse.

It seemed to me, in short, that a poem by Bragdon, while it might easily show the poet's fancy, could not fail to show also the produce-broker's clumsiness of touch. His charm was the spontaneity of his spoken words, his enthusiastic personality disarming all criticism ; what the labored productions of his fancy might prove to be, I hardly dared think. It was this dread that induced me, upon receipt of the box, appalling in its bulk and unpleasantly suggestive of the departure to other worlds of the original con-

" BUT FINALLY I OPENED THE BOX "

signor, since it was long and deep like the outer oaken covering of a casket, to delay opening it for some days; but finally I nerved myself up to the duty that had devolved upon me, and opened the box.

It was full to overflowing with printed books in fine bindings, short tales in Bragdon's familiar hand in copy-books, manuscripts almost without number, three Russia-leather record-books containing, the title-page told me, that which I most dreaded to find, *The Poems of Thomas Bragdon*, and dedicated to " His Dearest Friend " —myself. I had no heart to read beyond the dedication that night, but devoted all my time to getting the contents of the box into my library, having done which I felt it absolutely essential to my happiness to put on my coat, and, though the night was stormy, to rush out into the air. I think I should have suffocated in an open field with those literary remains of Thomas Bragdon heaped about me that night.

On my return I went immediately to bed, feeling by no means in the mood to read *The Poems of Thomas Bragdon*. I tossed about through the night, sleeping little, and in the morning rose up unrefreshed, and set about the examination of the papers and books intrusted to my care by my departed friend. And oh, the stuff I found there! If I was depressed at starting in, I was stupefied when it was all over, for the collection was mystifying to the point that it stunned.

In the first place, on opening Volume I. of the *Poems of Thomas Bragdon*, the first thing to greet my eyes were these lines:

CÒNSTANCY

Often have I heard it said
That her lips are ruby-red:
Little heed I what they say,
I have seen as red as they.
Ere she smiled on other men,
Real rubies were they then.
But now her lips are coy and cold;
  To mine they ne'er reply;
And yet I cease not to behold
  The love-light in her eye:
Her very frowns are fairer far
Than smiles of other maidens are.

As I read I was conscious of having seen the lines somewhere before, and yet I could not place them for the moment. They certainly possessed merit, so much so, in fact, that I marvelled to think of their being Bragdon's. I turned the leaves further and discovered this :

DISAPPOINTMENT

Come to me, O ye children,
  For I hear you at your play,
And the questions that perplexed me
  Have vanished quite away.

The Poem of the Universe
  Nor rhythm has nor rhyme;
Some God recites the wondrous song,
  A stanza at a time.

I dwell not now on what may be;
  Night shadows o'er the scene;
But still my fancy wanders free
  Through that which might have been.

Two stanzas in the poem, the first and the last, reminded me, as did the lines on "Constancy," of something I had read be-

fore. In a moment I had placed the first as
the opening lines of Longfellow's "Children," and a search through my books
showed that the concluding verse was taken
bodily from Peacock's exquisite little poem
"Castles in the Air."

Despairing to solve the problem that now
confronted me, which was, in brief, what
Bragdon meant by bodily lifting stanzas
from the poets and making them over into
mosaics of his own, I turned from the
poems and cast my eyes over some of the
bound volumes in the box.

The first of these to come to hand was a
copy of *Hamlet*, bound in tree calf, the sole
lettering on the book being on the back, as
follows :

This I deemed a harmless bit of vanity,
and not necessarily misleading, since many
collectors of books see fit to have their own
names emblazoned on the backs of their
literary treasures ; but pray imagine my hor-
ror upon opening the volume to discover
that the name of William Shakespeare had
been erased from the title-page, and that of
Thomas Bragdon so carefully inserted that
except to a practised eye none would ever
know that the page was not as it had always
been. I must confess to some mirth when
I read that title-page :

HAMLET, PRINCE OF DENMARK

A Tragedy

BY

THOMAS BRAGDON, ESQUIRE

The conceit was well worthy of my late
friend in one of his most fanciful moods.
In other volumes the same substitution had

been made, so that to one not versed in literature it would have seemed as though "Thomas Bragdon, Esquire," had been the author not only of *Hamlet*, but also of *Vanity Fair*, *David Copperfield*, *Rienzi*, and many other famous works, and I am not sure but that the great problem concerning the "Junius Letters" was here solved to the satisfaction of Bragdon, if not to my own. There were but two exceptions in the box to the rule of substituting the name of Bragdon for that of the actual author; one of these was an Old Testament, on the fly-leaf of which Bragdon had written, "To my dear friend Bragdon," and signed "The Author." I think I should have laughed for hours over this delightful reminder of my late friend's power of imagination had not the second exception come almost immediately to hand—a copy of Milton, which I recognized at once as one I had sent Tom at Christmas two years before his death, and on the fly-leaf of which I had written, "To Thomas Bragdon, with the love of, his faithfully, Philip Marsden." This was, indeed, a commonplace enough inscription, but it gathered unexpected force when I turned over a leaf and my eyes rested on the title, where Bragdon's love of substitutes had led him to put my name where Milton's had been.

The discovery was too much for my equanimity. I was thoroughly disconcerted, almost angry, and I felt, for the first time in my life, that there had been vagaries in Bragdon's character with which I could not entirely sympathize; but in justice to myself, it must be said, these sentiments were induced by first thoughts only. Certainly there could be but one way in which Bragdon's substitution of my name for Milton's could prove injurious or offensive to me who was his friend, and that was by his putting that copy out before the world to be circulated at random, which avenue to my discomfiture he had effectually closed by leaving the book in my hands, to do with it whatsoever I pleased. Second thoughts showed me that it was only a fear of what the outsider might think that was responsible for my temporary disloyalty to my departed comrade's memory, and then when I remembered how thoroughly we twain had despised the outsider, I was so ashamed of my aberration that I immediately renewed my allegiance to the late King Tom; so heartily, in fact, that my emotions wellnigh overcame me, and I found it best to seek distractions in the outer world.

I put on my hat and took a long walk along the Riverside Drive, the crisp air of the winter night proving a tonic to my disturbed system. It was after midnight when I returned to my apartment in a tolerably comfortable frame of mind, and yet as I opened the door to my study I was filled with a vague apprehension—of what I could not determine, but which events soon justified, for as I closed the door behind me, and turned up the light over my table, I became conscious of a pair of eyes fixed upon me. Nervously whirling about in my chair and glancing over towards my fireplace, I was for a moment transfixed with terror, for there, leaning against the mantel and gazing sadly into the fire, was Tom Bragdon himself—the man whom but a short time before I had seen lowered into his grave.

"GAZING INTO THE FIRE WAS TOM BRAGDON"

"Tom," I cried, springing to my feet and rushing towards him—"Tom, what does this mean? Why have you come back from the spirit world to—to haunt me?"

As I spoke he raised his head slowly until his eyes rested full upon my own, whereupon he vanished, all save those eyes, which remained fixed upon mine, and filled with the soft, affectionate glow I had so often seen in them in life.

"Tom," I cried again, holding out my hand towards him in a beseeching fashion, "come back. Explain this dreadful mystery if you do not wish me to lose my senses."

And then the eyes faded from my sight, and I was alone again. Horrified by my experience, I rushed from the study into my bedroom, where I threw myself, groaning, upon my couch. To collect my scattered senses was of difficult performance, and when finally my agitated nerves did begin to assume a moderately normal state, they were set adrift once more by Tom's voice, which was unmistakably plain, bidding me to come back to him there in the study.

Fearful as I was of the results, I could not but obey, and I rose tremblingly from my bed and tottered back to my desk, to see Bragdon sitting opposite my usual place just as he had so often done when in the flesh.

"Phil," he said in a moment, "don't be afraid. I couldn't hurt you if I would, and you know—or if you don't know you ought to know—that to promote your welfare has always been the supremest of my desires. I have returned to you here to-night to explain my motive in making the alterations in those books, and to account for the peculiarities of those verses. We have known each other, my dear boy, how many years?"

"Fifteen, Tom," I said, my voice husky with emotion.

"Yes, fifteen years, and fifteen happy years, Phil. Happy years to me, to whom the friendship of one who understood me was the dearest of many dear possessions. From the moment I met you I felt I had at last a friend, one to whom my very self might be confided, and who would through all time and under all circumstances prove true to that trust. It seemed to me that you were my soul's twin, Phil, and as the years passed on and we grew closer to each other, when the rough corners of my nature adapted themselves to the curves of yours, I almost began to think that we were but one soul united in all things spiritual, two only in matters material. I never spoke of it to you; I thought of it in communion with myself; I never thought it necessary to speak of it to you, for I was satisfied that you knew. I did not realize until — until that night a fortnight since, when almost without warning I found myself on the threshold of the dark valley, that perhaps I was mistaken. I missed you, and so sudden was the attack, and so swiftly did the heralds of death intrude upon me, that I had no time to summon you, as I wished; and as I lay there upon my bed, to the watchers unconscious, it came to me, like a dash of cold water in my face, that after all we were not one, but in reality two; for had we been one, you would have known of the perilous estate of your other self, and would have been with me at the last. And, Phil, the realization that chilled my very soul, that showed me that what I most dearly loved to believe was founded in unreality, reconciled me to the journey I was about to take into other worlds, for I knew that should I recover, life could never seem quite the same to me."

Here Bragdon, or his spirit, stopped speaking for a moment, and I tried to say something, but could not.

"I know how you feel, Phil," said he, noticing my discomfiture, "for, though you are not so much a part of me that you thoroughly comprehend me, I have become so much a part of you that your innermost thoughts are as plain to me as though they were mine. But let me finish. I realized when I lay ill and about to die that I had permitted my theory of happiness to obscure my perception of the actual. As you know, my whole life has been given over to imagination—all save that portion of my existence, which I shall not dignify by calling life, when I was forced by circumstances to .bring myself down to realities. I did not live whilst in commercial pursuits. It was only when I

could leave business behind and travel in
fancy wheresoever I wished that I was happy, and in those moments, Phil, I was full of
aspiration to do those things for which nature had not fitted me, and to the extent
that I recognized my inability to do those
things I failed to be content. I should have
liked to be a great writer, a poet, a great
dramatist, a novelist—a little of everything
in the literary world. I should have liked
to know Shakespeare, to have been the
friend of Milton; and when I came out of
my dreams it made me unhappy to think
that such I never could be, until one day
this idea came to me: all the happiness of
life is bound up in the 'let's pretend' games
which we learn in childhood, and no harm
results to any one. If I can imagine myself
off with my friend Phil Marsden in the lakes
of England and Scotland, in the African jun-
gle, in the moon, anywhere, and enter so far
into the spirit of the trips as to feel that
they are real and not imagination, why may
I not in fancy be all these things that I so
aspire to be? Why may not the plays of
Shakespeare become the plays of Thomas

Bragdon? Why may not the poems of Milton become the poems of my dearest, closest friend Phil Marsden? What is to prevent my achieving the highest position in letters, art, politics, science, anything, in imagination? I acted upon the thought, and I found the plan worked admirably up to a certain point. It was easy to fancy myself the author of *Hamlet* until I took my copy of that work in hand to read, and then it would shock and bring me back to earth again to see the name of another on the title-page. My solution of this vexatious complication was soon found. Surely, thought I, it can harm no one if I choose in behalf of my own conceit to substitute my name for that of Shakespeare, and I did so. The illusion was complete; indeed, it became no illusion, for my eyes did not deceive me. I saw what existed: the title-page of *Hamlet* by Thomas Bragdon. I carried the plan further, and where I found a piece of literature that I admired, there I made the substitution of my name for that of the real author, and in the case of that delightful copy of Milton you gave me, Phil,

it pleased me to believe that it was presented to me by the author, only the inscription
on the title-page made it necessary for me
to foist upon you the burden or distinction
of authorship. Then, as I lived on in my
imaginary paradise, it struck me that for one
who had done such great things in letters I
was doing precious little writing, and I bethought me of a plan which a dreadful reality made all the more pleasing. I looked
into literature to a slight extent, and I perceived at once that originality is no longer
possible. The great thoughts have been
thought; the great truths have been grasped
and made clear; the great poems have been
written. I saw that the literature of to-day is
either an echo of the past or a combination
of the ideas of many in the productions of
the individual, and upon that basis I worked.
My poems are combinations. I have taken
a stanza from one poet, and combining it
with a stanza from another, have made the
resulting poem my own, and in so far as I
have made no effort to profit thereby I have
been clear in my conscience. No one has
been deceived but myself, though I saw with

some regret this evening when you read my lines that you were puzzled by them. I had believed that you understood me sufficiently to comprehend them."

Here my ghostly visitor paused a moment and sighed. I felt as though some explanation of my lack of comprehension early in the evening was necessary, and so I said:

"I should have understood you, Tom, and I do now, but I have not the strength of imagination that you have."

"You are wrong there, Phil," said he. "You have every bit as strong an imagination as I, but you do not keep it in form. You do not exercise it enough. How have you developed your muscles? By constant exercise. The imagination needs to be kept in play quite as much as the muscles, if we do not wish it to become flabby as the muscles become when neglected. That your imagination is a strong one is shown by my presence before you to-night. In reality, Phil, I am lying out there in Greenwood, cold in my grave. Your imagination places me here, and as applied to my books, the play of *Hamlet* by Thomas Bragdon, and my poems, they will also demonstrate to you the strength of your fancy if you will show them, say, to your janitor, to-morrow morning. Try it, Phil, and see ; but this is only a part, my boy, of what I have come here to say to you. I am here, in the main, to show you that throughout all eternity happiness may be ours if we but take advantage of our fancy. Do you take delight in my society ? Imagine me present, Phil, and I will be present. There need be no death for us, there need be no separation throughout all the years to come, if you but exercise your fancy in life, and when life on this earth ends, then shall we be reunited according to nature's laws. Good-night, Phil. It is late ; and while I could sit here and talk forever without weariness, you, who have yet to put off your mortal limitations, will be worn out if I remain longer."

We shook hands affectionately, and Bragdon vanished as unceremoniously as he had appeared. For an hour after his departure I sat reflecting over the strange events of the evening, and finally, worn out in body and mind, dropped off into sleep. When I

awakened it was late in the forenoon, and I
was surprised when I recalled all that I had
gone through to feel a sense of exhilaration.
I was certainly thoroughly rested, and cares
which had weighed rather heavily on me in
the past now seemed light and inconsider-
able.   My apartments never looked so at-
tractive, and on my table, to my utter surprise and delight, I saw several objects of
art, notably a Baryé bronze, that it had been
one of my most cherished hopes to possess.
Where they came from I singularly enough
did not care to discover; suffice it to say
that they have remained there ever since,
nor have I been at all curious to know to
whose generosity I owe them, though when
that afternoon I followed Bragdon's advice,
and showed his book of poems and the
volume of *Hamlet* to the janitor, a vague
notion as to how matters really stood entered my mind.   The janitor cast his eye
over the leather-covered book of poems
when I asked what he thought of it.

"Nothin' much," he said. " You goin' to
keep a diary?"

"What do you mean?" I asked.

"'YOU GOIN' TO KEEP A DIARY?'"

"Why, when I sees people with handsome blank-books like that I allus supposes that's their object."

Blank-book indeed! And yet, perhaps, he was not wrong. I did not question it, but handed him the Bragdon *Hamlet.*

"Read that page aloud to me," I said, indicating the title-page and turning my back upon him, almost dreading to hear him speak.

"Certainly, if you wish it; but aren't you feeling well this morning, Mr. Marsden?"

"Very," I replied, shortly. "Go on and read."

"Hamlet, Prince of Denmark," he read, in a halting sort of fashion.

"Yes, yes; and what else?" I cried, impatiently.

"A Tragedy by William Shak—"

That was enough for me. I understood Tom, and at last I understood myself. I grasped the book from the janitor's hands, rather roughly, I fear, and bade him begone.

The happiest period of my life has elapsed since then. I understand that some of my friends profess to believe me queer ; but I do not care.   I am content.

The world is practically mine, and Bragdon and I are always together.

THE END

Reprint Publishing

FOR PEOPLE WHO GO FOR ORIGINALS.

This book is a facsimile reprint of the original edition. The term refers to the facsimile with an original in size and design exactly matching simulation as photographic or scanned reproduction.

Facsimile editions offer us the chance to join in the library of historical, cultural and scientific history of mankind, and to rediscover.

The books of the facsimile edition may have marks, notations and other marginalia and pages with errors contained in the original volume. These traces of the past refers to the historical journey that has covered the book.

ISBN 978-3-95940-074-9

Facsimile reprint of the original edition
Copyright © 2015 Reprint Publishing
All rights reserved.

Made in
Germany

www.reprintpublishing.com

www.ingramcontent.com/pod-product-compliance
Lightning Source LLC
Chambersburg PA
CBHW072119020726
47501CB00003B/887